CHAPTER ONE

ALICE FORD OPENED the top drawer of the spare desk in the office, searched for a pen and found a bombshell.

With her temper tested because her entire team was late back from lunch, she was relegated to answering the telephone when she should at this very moment be leading a meeting on how to move forward with the biggest account Innova Brand Management had yet won.

Add to that the absence of her own work station with its colour-coordinated filing system, pen pot, To-Do list and diary managing every moment of her day. This desk was a paper-strewn, disorganised mess from hell, used as a dumping ground for filing by everyone else in the place. Not a pen in sight, hence the need to claw through goodness knew what in the rubbish-filled drawers just so she could note down a phone message. There were crumbs under her fingernails. Bleurgh. And then exasperation spilled over as she looked in disbelief at the crumpled sheet of paper in her hands.

An innocent-at-first-glance grid. Columns filled out with the names of colleagues, amounts of money. Understanding kicked in, swiftly followed by irritation. Why was she even surprised?

Yet another office betting ring.

Seriously, what was it going to take to instil a proper work ethic into these people? Leading by example clearly wasn't enough. She ran a sensibly short and neutrally lacquered nail down the list of names. The whole office wasn't here, not by a long stretch, but all the usual suspects were. Exclusively male. Obviously feeling the need to confirm their masculinity by indulging in this kind of primitive-caveman pastime.

She wondered what it was this time. Maybe something to do with Roger from Accounts—she'd heard he was giving up smoking again. Too much to hope that it might be in aid of a charitable cause.

Then she caught sight of the few sentences at the top of the page and sudden cold horror flushed through her, accompanied by the disorienting sick sensation of sliding backwards in time. The heat of humiliation rose in her cheeks.

'Who can land Ice-Queen Ford? Proof required. In event of a tie, cash prize to be split equally.'

Alice swallowed hard and dug her nails hard into her palms until the prick of furious tears at the back of her throat subsided. Two things were clear:

Her male colleagues were betting on the dismal state of her love life, staking money on who could successfully have a crack at her.

The reputation she'd thought she held here was non-existent.

Far from being perceived as someone to look up to, she was apparently viewed as a dried-up frigid old spinster, enough of a challenge to wager money on, the perfect butt of a joke. Proof required? What the hell would that consist of? An item of underwear?

Humiliation had been long dead and resigned to the past, so she'd thought. But after three years of self-inflicted singledom, during which she'd taken control of every tiny facet of her life and had reinvented herself as career-woman-extraordinaire with no room on her list of priorities for a

About Charlotte Phillips

Charlotte Phillips has been reading romantic fiction since her teens, and she adores upbeat stories with happy endings. Writing them for Mills & Boon® is her dream job.

She combines writing with looking after her fabulous husband, two teenagers, a four-year-old and a dachshund. When something has to give, it's usually housework.

She lives in Wiltshire.

'If you're thinking about dating again, maybe you'd like to go for a drink,' he said.

'With you?'

The question exploded from her lips in the form of a laugh. Because it *was* laughable, wasn't it? That after her past experiences she would look twice at someone like him?

'Your amusement could be construed as an insult, you know,' he said mildly.

'I can't,' she said. 'Sorry.'

In Harry Stephens's world, of course, *no* meant *maybe*. He realised it was a simple matter of finding the right approach. Start small. And, most important of all, offer some kind of incentive. Make her think he could be part of the solution instead of part of the problem.

'Just hear me out,' he said. 'I've got a proposition for you.'

'What kind of proposition?'

The upset tone had slipped from her voice. He could almost hear the ticking over of her mind. Her attention had been raised because he'd given his question a detached work-style tone.

'I'm exactly what you need,' he said. 'To help you get back out there.'

All Bets Are On

Charlotte Phillips

First published in Great Britain 2013
by Mills & Boon, an imprint of Harlequin (UK) Limited.
Harlequin (UK) Limited, Eton House, 18-24 Paradise Road,
Richmond, Surrey TW9 1SR

© Charlotte Phillips 2013

ISBN: 978 0 263 23531 9

Harlequin (UK) policy is to use papers that are natural, renewable and recyclable products and made from wood grown in sustainable forests. The logging and manufacturing process conform to the legal environmental regulations of the country of origin.

Printed and bound in Great Britain
by CPI Antony Rowe, Chippenham, Wiltshire

Also by Charlotte Phillips

The Proposal Plan
Secrets of the Rich & Famous

**Did you know these are also available as eBooks?
Visit www.millsandboon.co.uk**

TM

*This book is for Libby, gorgeous daughter,
lovely friend and expert brainstormer.
With all my love.*

man, it seemed humiliation was alive and well and living in London.

Alice Ford was gossip-central.

Again.

Harry Stephens glanced around the bar, having just bought a round of drinks for the entire team. *Correction.* Almost the entire team. Despite the graft she'd put in to win the prestigious new contract, Alice Ford was a no-show yet again.

He finished his drink quickly and made his way across the bar, nodding at colleagues along the way. Fortunately Arabella had chosen to sit at a table close to the door. Perfect for the swift exit he intended to make the instant he finished speaking.

'Harry!' she said with real pleasure as he approached, loudly enough to draw glances from adjacent tables. The three other junior assistants sitting with her looked his way with interest. He was dimly aware that the redhead to Arabella's left must be new. Worth a second look, just not today. He filed her away in his mind for future consideration.

Arabella ran her fingers through her long blonde hair, twirling the ends lightly as she smiled at him. He kept his eyes on her face. The expression of adoration wasn't the only thing putting him on edge. The half-dozen texts she'd sent him so far today also needed to be considered along with the following facts:

1. she'd only left his bed at seven a.m.,

2. it was still only lunchtime, and

3. they worked in the same building.

The increasingly urgent texts along with the smile told him all he needed to know. It might have only been one night, but it was still time to jump ship.

Best to do it quick. Short, clean break before she had the chance to big it up in her mind into more than it was. Just sex. Just fun. No letting it run on too long—that led to all kinds of trouble as he'd recently discovered. And he was having none of it.

Keeping his voice deliberately detached, he reached into his inside jacket pocket.

'Sorry to interrupt,' he said. 'You left your earrings at my place.'

He held them out, found this morning in his bathroom. She didn't take them, a light frown touching the perfectly arched eyebrows.

'I know,' she said. 'I realised when I got to work. I just thought I'd pick them up next time I saw you. Maybe to-night—did you get my texts…?'

She trailed off, eyes fixed on his face, and he literally saw the click, saw her face begin to redden as she caught on. She wouldn't be visiting his place again. Her time there was done.

Smile gone now, she stood up, pushed past the redhead and joined him a few feet away by the door.

He held out the earrings again and this time she took them. She looked back up at him with a confident smile that was a bit too small to be pulled off.

'What's going on, Harry?'

He made his voice light, surprised.

'Nothing's going on. Last night was fun but I told you, I'm not interested in anything serious right now. I think it's best if we just call it quits, go back to being workmates.' He paused. 'Friends.'

He could tell from her face that 'friends' was going to be a bit of a big ask. All smiles had gone.

'You're dumping me? After one night?'

He heard the crack in her voice. He was so right to get out now.

'We both knew it was just a laugh,' he said.

Her gutted expression told him that *he* might have known

that, but she'd had much bigger plans. She opened her mouth, undoubtedly to argue the point further and he cut in quickly. Getting into a debate was a bad move; he knew that from experience.

He gave her upper arm a friendly squeeze, making sure he was well clear of her personal space.

'I'd better get back to the office,' he said. 'Thanks for a great night.'

He left quickly, secure in the knowledge that he'd been honest. He was not responsible for Arabella's feelings. He'd been up front with her from the start, made no promises, had made it crystal clear at all times where they both stood.

The fact she'd read more into the situation was nothing to do with him.

The outside line began ringing on various phones across the deserted office, but Alice was oblivious to the noise. Her eyes slipped to the bottom of the paper and her stomach gave another sickening lurch.

Page One.

There's more than one page?

She turned the paper over. Blank on the reverse. Next moment she was scrabbling through the desk, pulling out armfuls of papers, food wrappers, a half-eaten decaying sandwich. Her stomach gave a sickening lazy roll as she threw it on the floor. If there was a second page, if there were more people involved, she would damn well know about it.

Perspiration laced her forehead and upper lip as she stood back, out of breath, hands on hips. The desk drawers were empty, their contents strewn over the floor.

Nothing. Maybe this was it. As if it were enough.

She reread the list, and the wave of upset that she had managed to control until now crested with full force. Names that she dealt with on a daily basis, people she'd believed she had a friendly, trustworthy, albeit *working* relationship with. People she'd thought liked and respected her. She'd come all this way, put the past behind her, rebuilt herself from the inside out, and now she was a laughing stock again.

The bitterness that flooded her mouth tasted just the same. Back then it had been her own image, plastered on the internet, bandied about between so-called friends. This time she was the subject of a bet. Same difference. Three years ago or present day, she was the butt of other people's amusement.

The names blurred as tears came in a rush of uncontrollable sobs.

Across the open-plan room, the lift suddenly rumbled into life.

She snapped her head back up mid-sob, heart thundering in panic. In that brief moment it seemed entirely possible that the whole team, some thirty-odd people, were about to pour back in and find Alice a blubbering wreck with her head in her hands and a face full of snot, crumpled in the middle of the office.

The mortification of moments before stepped up to even dizzier heights.

She needed to get out of here. She did *not* need to be seen having an emotional meltdown by her colleagues. She needed a quiet space to think, calm down, get her head together. She stared madly around the room and finally made a manic dash for the only option of refuge within sprinting distance.

Sad cliché that it was, Alice Ford, top-class ambitious professional, was about to be reduced to crying in the Ladies.

Stumbling blindly between desks, knocking her thigh agonisingly hard against the corner of the printer table and upending a bin as she went, she sprinted in her high-heeled court shoes towards the door of the restroom, actually had it in her sights as the ping of the lift signalled its arrival and the doors slid smoothly apart.

She almost made it. A second or two faster and all Harry Stephens would have known about it would have been the slamming of the door behind her. Instead what he got was a full-on glimpse of her face as she shoved past him. Since the first thing she saw as she made it into the Ladies was her own reflection in the mirror, she knew that, humiliatingly, he'd just been treated to her beetroot-red face running with a combination of tears and snot and her always-sleek chignon looking like a rat's nest where she'd been clutching in anguish at her hair.

A loud knock on the door made her jump.

'Alice?'

She ignored him.

'Alice?' Louder this time. 'Are you OK?'

Another knock. Perhaps if she kept quiet he'd give up. She clutched the side of the sink in frustration.

'Sandra's downstairs in Reception. I'll go and get her,' he said.

Sandra. The resentful marketing assistant who'd been passed over when Alice got her promotion to Account Manager and who would probably like to see her buried under a patio. No, thanks. She could envisage the ill-hidden glee and fake concern on Sandra's face right now and it was enough to galvanise her into action.

'I am fine!' she snapped, hearing the nasal tone in her voice from all the crying and hating it. 'I don't need Sandra or anyone else. I'm perfectly all right.'

He totally ignored her.

'No, you're not. What's up? Maybe I can help?'

The idea that she might want an emotional chat about her love life, or lack of it, with the man who was sleeping his way through the office actually raised a crazy bubble of laughter.

'Go away,' she snapped.

'I'm not going anywhere until I know you're OK.'

The concern that softened the deep voice was, of course, not genuine. Harry Stephens didn't do concern. As Head of Graphic Design he did creative brilliance in the office and short-term devastation in his personal life. Emotions like concern need not apply. Anyone with a pulse and a pretty face in this building had probably at some point looked into his deep blue eyes and thought he would be different with her. So far, he never had been.

She was just trying to come up with an adequately cutting response that would get him off her case once and for all when he opened the door. She hadn't considered for one second that he'd actually have the arrogance to follow her into the ladies' room. She caught a glimpse of her own gobsmacked expression in the mirror as she dashed into one of the cubicles and twisted the lock.

'You can't come in here!' she squawked.

'I'm already in here,' he said. A pause. 'And I'm not going anywhere until I know you're OK, so you might as well just come out with it.'

She heard the squeak of the wicker chair in the corner as he made himself comfortable. Despair rushed in and buried her. She'd let her guard down; let the mess she'd been in the past show through. And he'd seen it. The real Alice Ford—behind the iron-solid professional glossy persona she'd worked so hard to perfect.

The surge of grief swelled back up, too big to squash down or bat aside, and in her misery her guard slipped a little.

She sat down on the toilet, clutched her hot forehead in her hands, and closed her eyes against her wet palms. She had the beginnings of a headache.

'It's nothing,' she mumbled. 'Work stuff.'

A vague comment that would probably put most people off probing any further, Harry thought. She was the expert at keeping things on a work level. He couldn't think of a single person in the office who had ever socialised properly with her.

He wasn't most people.

'Then I can definitely help,' he said. 'If it's work related. I'm always happy to help out a colleague.'

'Please will you just go away?'

The despair in her voice tugged unexpectedly at his heart. He jumped a little in surprise. Of course, he didn't *do* crying women so no wonder his reactions were off kilter. He didn't need emotional angst. Avoid like the plague.

Except that this situation was also an *opportunity.*

Alice Ford was the current subject of the office betting ring, an outwardly light-hearted but in reality deadly serious pastime. Naturally he had a huge stake in it and naturally he intended to win. He'd simply been biding his time. And now that time was here.

'No chance,' he said.

He heard her strangled sob and was on his feet before he knew what he was doing, moving across to the cubicle door. He spoke through it, making his voice gentle.

'Come on. Tell me what's up,' he encouraged. 'Is it family stuff? I know what that can be like.' He certainly did. Putting family stuff out of his mind was pretty much up there at the top of his priorities.

'No,' she mumbled, between sobs.

'Boyfriend stuff, then?'

A perfunctory suggestion and he knew it. The word was that there had been no boyfriend in years—the surprisingly high-stakes bet proved that. But no harm in confirming the fact, confirming the *challenge.*

'You don't know the first thing about it!' she howled angrily through the door. 'With your life-is-a-cabaret attitude.'

'Oh, OK, so tell me the first thing about it. Has some bloke dumped you? Because if he has, he's an idiot.'

In Harry's opinion, flattery was always a good starting point.

She snorted bitterly.

'Are you having some kind of a laugh?'

'No. I just assumed that the main reason women cry in toilets is over men.'

'Well, of course, you'd know that, wouldn't you? I bet there have been plenty of tears shed in here over you.'

He chose to ignore that.

'If it's not over a man, then what the hell is it?'

'Will you please just leave me alone?' The anguished note rose in her voice. Maybe if he just pushed her a bit harder.

'No. Not until you tell me what's wrong.'

The answer came in a sobbing shout and the cubicle door rattled as if she'd beat a fist against it. He stepped back in surprise.

'All right, then, it *is* over men! *Plural!* Not just one man, the whole damn lot of you! You think I'm having a meltdown because some bloke's dumped me? I haven't dated in three years. Go on and laugh it up now!'

She dissolved into a flurry of sobs again, coming up every so often to blurt out more details.

'It's not that I don't want to date, it's just been so long I haven't a clue where to start. I can't face the whole night-mare of meeting a guy, investing all that emotion, all that time and energy, only to be kicked in the teeth a few months down the line.' A sob. 'I'll be single for ever and end up one of those women in a houseful of cats smelling of wee.' A loud snuffle followed by a furious snarl. 'And my clock is ticking!' Another sob, tapering off into sniffles.

He took a moment to consider how best to play this. He couldn't quite believe his luck. By pure coincidence he'd happened to come back to the office early, find her like this and now here it suddenly was. The chance he needed.

Insider knowledge.

A way into her life where he could then stay put long enough to win the bet and scoop the cash and the kudos.

This year or so in London, the job here, were beginning to pay dividends. Finally a sense of freedom. New place, new people. After the last few weeks he was definitely ready for a new challenge. Arabella had just been a diversion. This would be something else entirely. It was common knowledge that Alice was a workaholic who kept all men at arm's length. Now he knew that wasn't what she *really* wanted, he could use the fact to his advantage. She was just too used to being single; that was all it was.

She needed some persuasion.

'Alice, listen to me,' he began.

His voice was gentle and kind, and Alice's stomach gave a sudden melty flip-flop. Apparently even in the depths of emotional meltdown her body was as receptive to his charm as the rest of the female workforce, who cared only that he looked like an Adonis with his dark-hair-blue-eyes combo and the muscular build and leftover tan from whatever sporty summer holiday he'd taken.

Fortunately she was able to rely on her mind, which knew only too well the kind of man he was.

'You just need to get out more, that's all,' he said, jump-starting her temper, which up to now had been squashed into submission by humiliation and disbelief. She unwound a huge wad of toilet roll and wiped her eyes angrily.

'I need to get out more?' she snapped through the door. The simplicity of the suggestion, pigeon-holing all her problems into one easy sentence, infuriated her. 'Like you, you mean? Your social life is the talk of the post room. You must be barely ever home. I'm surprised you're able to fit work in. Don't you ever wonder what the point of it all is?'

There was a surprised silence.

'The point is to have fun,' he said. 'Look, I'm not trying to criticise. I'm just saying that the sun doesn't rise and set with Innova. When did you last go out? Socially, I mean. For a drink or a meal?'

'I go out,' she said defensively, glaring at the back of the cubicle door, imagining him on the other side of it, with his dark tousled hair, crinkly-eyed smile, and his endless string of girlfriends and rampant social life. An image of her own previous evening flashed into her mind. Herself on the sofa, Kevin the cat on one side, stack of work files on the other, laptop open, *CSI* box set on the TV in the background. Hell, it might as well be an image of any evening this week. This year.

'When? Where? Who with?'

'What are you, my father? I *see* people.' She frowned indignantly at the closed door.

'See me, then,' he said in a low voice and that soft melty sensation bubbled hotly back up inside her. She slid her hands across her middle and pressed hard to make it stop as she groped for a suitable response. Any response.

'Alice?' he said. Her stupid heart had begun to beat madly. She took a deep calming breath.

'What?'

His voice was low and close. She knew he must be literally right on the other side of the door.

'If you haven't dated for a long time and you're thinking of getting back out there—'

'I didn't say that!' she snapped. Oh, what the hell was she thinking, blurting out all her problems to him? At best he could go back to the office and report that Ice-Queen Ford was having a crying fit over being perpetually single.

At worst, there really might be a Page Two of the damn bet pool and Harry Stephens could be right there on it with a big fat stake.

His voice was serious though, steady, making her feel as if he could see perfectly well through her bravado. Her insides felt suddenly squiggly.

'Because if you were…'

'Were what?'

Her thumping heart seemed to be working independently of her mind.

Please. Was she actually having a swooning moment over Harry Stephens of all people? After all she'd been through in the past had her body learned *nothing*? Did her heart have no reservations about reacting to the most unreliable playboy bachelor London had ever seen? Over the past year or so, he'd had more female workers in tears than she'd had hot coffees! She gritted her teeth. Obviously she'd been thrown off balance by discovery of the bet. Her usual defences had been scrambled.

'If you were thinking about dating again, maybe you'd like to go for a drink,' he said.

'With you?'

The question exploded from her lips in the form of a laugh. Because it was laughable, wasn't it? That after her past experiences she would look twice at someone like him.

'Your amusement could be construed as an insult, you know,' he said mildly.

'I can't,' she said. 'Sorry.'

Stock answer. No excuse required. Always worked on the run-of-the-mill guys in the office, those that dared broach the aloof distance she kept between herself and her colleagues. She could count the times she'd been asked out at work on one hand and, come to think of it, two of them had been in the last month or so. Her cheeks flushed hotly. Now she knew why—because there was a pot of cash waiting to be scooped by the man who managed to land her. She wondered again if Harry was involved.

'Of course you can,' he said. 'No one works twenty-four-seven. Not even you. It's only a drink. An hour. Everyone has an hour.'

'I'm busy,' she said again. 'I don't date.'

In Harry Stephens's world, of course, no meant maybe. He realised it was a simple matter of finding the right approach. One that might *appeal* to her reluctance to get out there instead of feeding it. Start small. If she hadn't dated for years, more than a drink or a coffee was going to seem monumental. And most important of all, offer some kind of incentive.

Make her think he could be part of the solution instead of part of the problem.

'Just hear me out,' he said. 'I've got a proposition for you.'

'What kind of proposition?'

The upset tone had slipped from her voice. He could almost hear the ticking over of her mind, her attention raised because he'd given his question a detached work-style tone.

'I'm exactly what you need,' he said. 'To help you get back out there.'

CHAPTER TWO

THERE WAS A snap as the lock twisted back on the cubicle door and then Alice was in front of him. The tears had dried and her face was no longer purple. She looked pale and tired, her eyes red-rimmed from all the crying. Her hair, still partially twisted into its chignon, stuck out at odd angles. She took a deliberate side-step around him and moved across to the sink, putting a good space between them. Harry saw her grimace at her own reflection before she turned her gaze back on him.

As her eyes narrowed a spark of sudden heat zipped up his spine. Obviously because Alice Ford didn't do vulnerable, he decided, that was all. She did polished and professional. He was bound to react to such a change in her.

'What do you mean, you're exactly what I need?'

Her arms were crossed defensively, her face totally suffused with suspicion and he knew that convincing her he was genuine was going to be tough. Then again, tough had never caused him a problem before.

'What if I were to offer you my services?' he said.

She was looking at him as if she thought he might be crazy.

'Your services? As what exactly?'

He shrugged, leaned back against the wall and looked her in the eye.

'As someone who dates a lot. Someone who's out there.'

He ignored the cynical expression on her face and forged ahead.

'Instead of going to bars or restaurants on your own, come out with me. You said yourself just now, you're rusty. And starting from scratch at anything is pretty daunting—right? Just think of the alternatives.' He shrugged. 'There's internet dating, where you never know if the person showing up is a serial killer.'

'As opposed to a serial dater,' she said, eyebrows raised.

'Hey, that's an advantage! I've probably been on more first dates than anyone else you know. I'm used to the social scene. I know all the best places to go to meet new people. I'm perfect for the job. Whatever your reason is for staying out of the field these last three years, whatever moron has stitched you up or treated you badly in the past—'

'How do you know that's the reason?' she snapped, his interest sharpening at her sudden defensiveness. 'I've been putting work first, that's all. Focusing on my career. It's as simple as that. I don't need your help.'

'OK, OK.' He held his hands up. 'You've still been out of the field for a while. Out of the social scene, out of the habit of getting to know people.'

'I get to know people!' she protested.

He deliberately fixed his gaze on hers.

'Professionally maybe. But what about getting to know someone for pleasure?'

He saw a soft blush touch the porcelain skin of her cheekbones. He had her on edge. He liked having that effect on her.

'Just think about it for a minute. A few no-strings dates with me and you'll have checked out a few nice bars, maybe a restaurant or two, you will have broken the ice, started talking to people about something other than work for a change.' He winked at her. 'You'll be back out there. Problem solved.'

He paused, then added an extra touch of encouragement. 'And no one needs to know we ever had this conversation.'

Momentary relief in her eyes as she picked up on that last sentence. And then a sceptical smile touched the corner of her mouth, drawing his attention there.

'And assuming I were to go along with this, what happens once I am "back out there"?'

He shrugged.

'Then, when it runs its course, we part company and you make your own way forward, back in full control.' He held his hands up in what he hoped was a you-can-trust-me gesture. 'Totally risk-free.'

She gave him an amused look from beneath her dark eyelashes and his pulse rate began to climb unexpectedly. When you bothered to look beyond the starchy business persona she really was a knockout. She just needed to loosen up a bit.

'Come on,' he persuaded. 'What have you got to lose?'

Her gaze narrowed suddenly.

'And what exactly is in it for you? Why the hell would you want to take me out when you have the pick of the office, not to mention the city? I'm sure HR are recruiting at the moment—there should be a whole new intake of candidates for you to hit on if you wait a week or two. You've never seemed to have a problem finding someone before. And judging by the trail of devastation you leave around the office they all seem to be a bit more into you than I am.'

He grinned.

'Maybe I like a challenge.'

She only looked at him levelly. How come he hadn't realised before how softly pretty she was? Her wide brown eyes were fringed with thick dark lashes contrasting richly with her creamy skin. The way she pulled her dark hair severely back from her face combined with the sharply tailored business suits she favoured made the overall impression coldly keep-your-distance professional, not pretty or sexy. Which, he realised, was probably the point.

'What about Angela? Or is it Emily?' She flung an exasperated hand up. 'That temp from Accounts.'

'I think you must mean Ellie,' he said. 'It's been over for a while. I've actually been out of the field myself this past month.'

He didn't count yesterday's one-night stand. Extra-short-term flings were the new thing.

She gave an amused sniff.

'Am I supposed to feel an affinity with that? A month is hardly an abstention, is it? It's more of a…breather.'

'OK, so it doesn't come close to your three-year cold spell,' he said, 'but it's still been a deliberate step back.'

He took a breath, the hassle of the last few weeks zipping spectacularly through his mind in a haze of all-night repetitive phone calls and shredded clothes. Thankfully it seemed to be over now and he'd learned from his mistakes. From now on, clear caveats up front and no letting it run on too long. More than a month seemed to be code for women that moving in together was a realistic next step.

He shrugged. 'Is it so unbelievable to you that I might want to take you out?'

Alice stared at him.

Actually, yes. Forgive me for being cautious but I have just discovered I'm the office joke.

'How come you haven't asked me out before, then?' she asked. 'Why now?'

'You do have a bit of a…well, a reputation.' He ran a hand through his dark hair, ruffling it, obviously struggling to put it tactfully.

She tensed. If he dared use the term 'Ice-Queen', murder might be on the cards.

'Oh, really?' she said.

'As being a bit aloof. But you must have been asked out before, surely?'

'A couple of times,' she said. 'A firm "no" has always been enough before.'

He grinned.

'I don't give up that easily. When I see something I want, I make sure I get it.'

She jumped a little at the muffled ping of the lift outside followed by a flurry of voices and footsteps. Her colleagues, pouring back into the office. She needed to regain her composure if she was going to go back out there. And if she wanted him to keep quiet about her little meltdown just now, it might pay to keep him onside.

Risk-free, he'd said. There was a small part of her that zoomed in on those two words.

Three years and she hadn't so much as been out for a coffee with a man. She had anticipated the day she agreed to a date again would be some kind of milestone. Broken heart fully healed. Pain resigned to the distant past along with sewer-rat Simon and his photographs. But now it seemed the last three years of swearing off the opposite sex had been totally pointless. She was in exactly the same place now as she had been then—the butt of amused gossip. This time because she didn't date instead of because she did.

Deep down her stomach twisted into agonising knots at the thought of putting herself back out there again. What the hell was wrong with staying in? She never got behind on any TV shows and it saved her a fortune in clothes.

The thought of going out with someone as dangerous as Harry Stephens was akin to playing with fire. But *risk-free*, he said.

In the face of the day she'd had, knowing how she was

viewed by the entire office, she could see that a date with him might have its merits. She had to do something. Even a stupid ego-boosting date with the office lothario was *something* if it was done on her terms. And since what she wanted was to prove a point, wasn't he the perfect choice? High profile in the circles she moved in. Gorgeous. And indiscreet—he wasn't above dumping his conquests in full view of the office, seeming to revel in his reputation as a player. He'd be bound to tell half the office that he'd been out for a drink with the Ice-Queen. That would throw a spanner in the works of their sad little sweepstake. And she could always back out later if she changed her mind.

She had a choice: end this day as Ice-Queen Ford or accept the offer of a drink and at least be able to tell herself she had a date, no matter that it was with the most unsuitable man in the universe.

'OK,' she said impulsively.

He looked momentarily surprised and she realised he hadn't really expected her to say yes. The idea that she was acting out of character spurred her on even more, offering a stab of what felt like excitement. Except it couldn't be, because she didn't *do* excitement.

Hah! Didn't expect that, did he? Didn't expect a yes from Ice-Queen Ford!

To his credit, he collected himself quickly.

'Great,' he said. 'After work?'

The sudden scary reality of what she was doing kicked in and she scrabbled for thinking time.

'Tonight's difficult,' she said. 'I'm cooking for my flatmate.' Never mind the fact that slave-to-the-ready-meal Tilly wouldn't give a damn if she changed her plans.

A muffled laugh from outside the room made her tense. Was this how it was going to be? Thinking every chuckle in the office, every whispered conversation was about her? Enough was enough.

'I'll check my diary and let you know,' she said.

'If it bothers you that much—which it must do because it's all you've talked about since you got home—give me one good reason why you aren't just taking it to the top and getting the whole damn lot of them fired or reprimanded, or whatever it is you do in an office environment?'

Besides sharing a childhood and now a flat with Alice, Tilly sold ethnic jewellery at various markets, dabbled in various other off-the-wall jobs and had an ongoing role as Alice's voice of reason. Now she pushed her chilli-pepper-red hair out of her eyes and leaned back against the kitchen counter while Alice put dinner together.

'Because then I'd have to hand this piece of paper over to my boss.' Alice brandished the betting pool under Tilly's nose.

Tilly pulled a face.

'Blimey, he's not on the list, is he?'

She shook her head. 'Not as far as I know. Thank goodness. At least there's one man in the building who isn't a chauvinist. But it would lead to a big investigation—I'd have to discuss it all in detail. I just can't face the embarrassment of it all.'

The thought of slipping this piece of paper in front of the CEO filled her with dark horror at the way it portrayed her. Not just the Ice-Queen comment, but the very fact her colleagues were betting on her behaviour. All her hard work to build the perfect corporate image obviously hadn't cut the mustard with her subordinates. All this time she'd been priding herself on the way her colleagues regarded her. But it was clear from this situation that she didn't command the slightest bit of respect and revealing that to her boss would only diminish her standing even further. It was like school all over again, picking your way through the years, trying to keep your head below the parapet so you didn't attract any unwanted attention.

Tilly pursed her lips, considering.

'You have a point. Plus you don't want the hideous creeps to think they've got to you.'

'Which they haven't.' Alice pointed the wooden spoon emphatically at Tilly, then went back to stirring the chilli con carne.

''Course they haven't, honey. So instead you handle this the only way you can.'

'Which is?'

'You have to see it as a sign, use it to your own advantage.' She waved her fingers in the air in an all-encompassing gesture.

Alice tried not to roll her eyes in exasperation. Did she have to put a mystic slant on everything?

'For Pete's sake, Tilly, don't ask me to see this as some kind of karma, some fatalistic indication from the gods.'

'Everything happens for a reason,' Tilly countered.

Alice sighed.

'OK, then, a sign of what?'

'That you need to actually *do* that thing you're always talking about but never do.'

'Which is?'

Tilly leaned forward. 'Get back out there. This whole bet is based on the fact you never so much as go for a drink with a guy. Ever. They see you as some power-suited, up-tight workaholic. That's what they've latched on to—that's the stick they're beating you with. Well, you've licked your wounds long enough. Get back on that dating horse, Ice-Queen, and prove that moronic bunch wrong. Stop procrastinating and go out with this guy from work.'

She folded her arms triumphantly. There were times when Alice wondered how on earth she and Tilly could be such good friends.

'I'm not ready,' she protested.

'You never are. But that's OK, there is one other option.'

Alice brightened immediately.

'What's that?'

'You could become a nun.'

'Very funny.'

'Look, you've said you want a family one day. That means at some point you're going to *have* to bite the bullet and date again. It might as well be now. This could be just the push you need. And this guy, this Harry, asked you out today.' She shrugged. 'So go out with him.' She winked at Alice. 'Or I could have a think if you prefer. Julian's bound to have a few single mates I could set you up with.'

Tilly's boyfriend, Julian, was a strict vegan who had actually done that experiment whereby if you ceased washing your hair it would eventually cease needing to be washed. The matted result hadn't convinced Alice to give up the shampoo and conditioner any time soon.

'Thanks but Julian's not…' She groped for a tactful description.

'Not really your type?' Tilly grinned. 'Then go out with this Harry from the office.'

'But he's exactly the kind of guy I wouldn't touch with a bargepole. He's broken more hearts than you've been to music festivals. Harry Stephens: King of the One-night Stand.'

'Sounds the perfect foil for an Ice-Queen,' Tilly said, snatching a bread roll from the worktop. 'And it certainly sounds like he's into you.'

Alice frowned.

'I'm not sure he's exactly into me, as you so classily put it. He offered me his services. As Serial Dater.'

'As what?'

Tilly looked mystified and Alice couldn't really blame her. It did sound ludicrous spoken out loud.

'When I knocked him back on just going out for a drink, he tried to sell it as helping me back into a social life. I think he sees it as some kind of personal glory trip, like he's mentoring me or something because I'm obviously socially inept. He's getting off on it, like some kind of dating fairy godfather.' She put a hand briefly over her eyes. 'It's almost too humiliating—the idea that he thinks I would need his input into my social life.'

'Well, you do,' Tilly said around a mouthful of bread. 'I thought that was a given. And you could do worse. A lot easier to start trying out the nightlife, eyeing up the talent, if you're on the arm of someone at the…you know…*hub* of it all. He'll know all the best places to go. You can really get your confidence up instead of sitting on your own in a corner with a mineral water waiting for someone to approach you. Someone totally unsuitable.'

Alice raised offended eyebrows. Tilly jabbed the roll at her.

'You do have a bit of a history.'

She had to concede Tilly had a point.

Tilly lobbed the remains of the roll in the bin and hoisted herself up to sit on the counter next to the hob.

'Go on. It'll be fun. And after this whole betting debacle, what the hell have you got to lose? Can a couple of dates make you feel more of a loser than you already do?'

'You're seriously testing our friendship here, you know.'

'I'm being honest with you like I always am. That's why you love me!'

Alice stirred the chilli. She had to admit Tilly had a point.

Every second of the rest of the day in the office had passed excruciatingly. The bet swamped her mind and she was filled with frustration, hating the fact that she couldn't face reporting them. Strong Alice Ford, who ate errant juniors for breakfast, couldn't take a bunch of men to task for messing about in work time at her expense. She had believed herself stronger, more rebuilt than that, and it had crushed her confidence more than she wanted to admit, even to Tilly.

'What if he's in on the bet too? Why else would he want to take me out?'

'Is it really so impossible to believe that he might just find you attractive?' Tilly said.

'I'm not the usual kind of girl he goes for.'

Tilly frowned.

'Maybe he's upping his game, then. Look, he wasn't on the list, was he? Are you sure you got a full copy of the names?'

She shook her head.

'I don't know… I tore the desk apart looking for a Page Two or, worse, Page Three. That one page is all there was. But I can't be sure. Even if I asked him he'd deny it.'

Tilly pursed her lips, considering.

'OK, forget about his motives for a second. Does it even *matter* whether he's in on the bet or not? Why not just look at what's in this for you? Like it or not, you really could do with his input. Don't you think the insights you could get from dating someone like him, from just watching his behaviour, might be valuable?'

And suddenly there it was.

A flash of inspiration that fell on her like a ton of bricks, a bucket of ice, a jolt of electricity. Not a foolproof way through the minefield that was dating, more an *approach* to it. One that appealed to her constant desire to be in control, to avoid the pitfalls she'd shown herself to be so susceptible to in the past.

'Erm, I think that might be burning,' Tilly said.

Alice suddenly realised the chilli was catching on the bottom and Tilly was staring at her. She shook herself and stirred it vigorously.

'I could use him to build up a profile,' she said, thinking out loud.

'A what?'

She looked at Tilly with sudden excitement.

'What if I could use him to come up with a behaviour profile? A list of the way players react in certain situations so I can identify that type of man in the future before I get in too deep? I can come up with a list from my own experiences, then test it on Harry. Think about it. Think how much a list like that would have helped me when I was going out with Simon—I would have recognised from the start what kind of man he was and I could have kicked him into touch way before any damage was done.' *And saved myself a whole lot of grief.*

'Harry Stephens is the embodiment of everything I need to avoid in a man.' She shrugged. 'Well, except for the chiselled face and super-fit body. He's the worst kind of player. He has zero regard for the women he takes out but he's so gorgeous that none of them are able to see past that. I've seen enough assistants crying into their coffee over him at work to know that. Well, I *can* see past that, and I can use him to build myself some dating criteria.'

Tilly was staring at her as if she might be mad.

'Oh, for crying out loud, you and your lists! You can't possibly be serious. This isn't the office—this is the real world. You can't run every facet of your life that way. It won't work.'

'It can't hurt. How hard can it be? All I have to do is go on a few dates.'

'While not falling for him. What *about* that chiselled face and super-fit body? The broad shoulders you told me about?

You can't backtrack now and tell me you don't find him attractive.'

'OK, he is attractive,' she conceded, rolling her eyes. 'But with his track record, falling for him is the last thing I'm going to do.'

Her mind was running with the idea now, trying to get it off the ground.

'I could take it step by step. How does a player behave on a first date? How long does it take him to call or text? That kind of thing.'

'When does he go for a first kiss? How long does he wait before he tries to get you into bed?' Tilly said.

Sudden heat curled up through Alice's body and pooled softly in her stomach at the thought. Since it had been three years since she'd had sex she cut her stupid overreacting body some slack and ignored it.

'I wasn't thinking so much about the physical side of dating,' she said through gritted teeth.

'Well, you'd better get started.'

Tilly jumped down from the counter and retrieved a bottle of wine from the fridge.

'Because you can bet whatever you like that the physical side of dating is exactly what *he's* thinking about.'

Harry found himself at the office brutally early for a change. Waking early, he had found sleep shoved aside by thoughts of uptight Alice with her work obsession and her challenging attitude. He wasn't about to be put off by a bit of procrastination. He sought her out at her desk, certain that she would be there despite the crushingly early hour, because she always was. He was right. Perfectly groomed as always, a takeaway coffee on one side of the pristine desk.

She glanced up as he approached.

'That drink,' she said, before he had the chance to get back in and start persuading. 'I've thought it over and I'd like to go, if the offer's still on.'

Bet your life the offer was still on.

He knew once he got her out and alone with him that he could convert the situation into whatever he wanted it to be. Yet the expected stab of triumph didn't for some reason materialise. After yesterday's coldness, the sudden change of heart was unexpected and he didn't miss the cautious tone of her voice or the way she fidgeted with the pen in her hand. He was struck again by how appealing he found her. Had she really not been out with a guy for three years? Despite the severe business dress and scraped-back hair, she was undeniably pretty and smart. What the hell had happened to her to make her withdraw like that?

''Course it's still on. Let me know your address and I'll pick you up.'

She held up a hand.

'Please, let me finish. First of all, we need to talk terms.'

Not such an easy victory after all, then.

'Terms?'

'Yes,' she said. She gave him a businesslike smile across the desk, pen twiddling between her fingers.

He felt a spark of amusement.

'You're going out on a date, not buying a car.'

She pursed her lips. He tried to drag his eyes away; the soft fullness of them was just delectable.

'True,' she said. 'But in my opinion there'd be a lot less heartbreak and the divorce rate would be a lot lower if people just took the time to negotiate terms a bit. Get it all sorted up front so everyone knows where they stand and there's no danger of misunderstandings. Ergo, no one gets hurt.' She pointed her pen at him. 'Someone like you could benefit a lot from terms, I think.'

'Someone like me?'

'Yes.' She looked up at him. 'A, you know, *player.*' She dropped her eyes quickly away from his and looked down at her desk.

'Is that what I am?' he said, biting back a smile.

She didn't look up.

'Did you or did you not hand back a pair of earrings to Arabella yesterday, pointing out that she'd left it at your place and making it clear she wouldn't be visiting you there again, thereby causing her to take sick leave for the day?'

Was this for real?

He inclined his head cautiously. 'OK, maybe I did.'

She nodded triumphantly.

'And so we have terms.'

A flash of exasperation made him wonder whether she might drive him nuts just over the course of an hour or so, let alone a series of dates. Was this really worthwhile for a bit of a laugh and a few hundred quid? She took high maintenance to the next level.

Higher maintenance.

Then his eyes dipped down again to her full lower lip and the determined look in the dark brown eyes and unexpected heat began to burn low in his abdomen.

It occurred to him that maybe just what he needed after the last month or so was an antidote to pushover. So she was difficult. So what? There were half a dozen girls he could call up right now who would fall at his feet. He couldn't be less interested in any of them. It seemed that wasn't what piqued his attention these days. Not any more. Easy was just…well, too damned easy. And easy led to a lot of hassle when it ended.

'Go on,' he said.

'Great!' She smiled up at him. 'Then let's be clear. This is just a few dates. Nothing serious. I won't be jumping into bed with you.' She held his gaze briefly before dropping her eyes. 'I'm not that kind of girl.'

So this was her setting up ground rules? He bit the inside of his mouth to suppress a grin.

'Sounds risk-free,' he said.

'It is.'

'Unless you fall for me.'

'That isn't going to happen. You are the exact opposite of the type of man I'm looking for. In the long term, I mean.'

She took a sip of her coffee.

'When you're back up to speed, so to speak.'

She nodded. 'Exactly. I've had enough of guys like you to last me a lifetime. I need a keeper.'

'A keeper,' he repeated.

'Yes. The polar opposite of player. Treats you with respect and isn't commitment-phobic.'

'I'll treat you with respect,' he protested.

'And the commitment part?'

He shrugged.

'Maybe thinking that far ahead just takes all the fun out of it.'

She gave him a dismissive smile that told him she couldn't agree less.

'I just want to be clear from the outset that this isn't going to get serious.'

If by serious she meant physical, he was confident he could turn that around. No need to argue the point now though—let her have it her way.

He held his hands up.

'Suits me fine.'

She examined her fingernails.

'You never know, I might even be able to give you a few pointers if you like. On how to treat women...you know... properly. On where you're going wrong.'

For a moment he couldn't quite believe his ears. Was she actually suggesting he needed dating advice?

'Where *I'm* going wrong? You're the one who's spent the last three years in the dating desert, not me.'

'That was by choice. I could have dated—I just didn't want to.'

'Why not?'

She dropped her eyes from his.

'None of your business,' she said.

Something must have happened. She'd been dumped badly, maybe cheated on. He wasn't about to press the point right now though, not when he almost had the date in the bag.

'No offence,' he said, 'but I don't need any pointers, thanks very much.'

She shrugged.

'Please yourself. But you can't deny some of your behaviour is a bit…'

'Detached?'

'Brutal. We've probably lost weeks of productivity with the amount of sick leave your broken hearts have caused around here.'

'That isn't my fault,' he protested. 'I make it clear from the outset I'm not interested in settling down. Can I be blamed when people read more into it than that?'

'We should get on perfectly, then. Neither of us wants anything serious.'

He held her gaze deliberately.

'You never know, you might find a player is more fun after all.'

He caught the blush again, high on her cheekbones. Nice.

'We'll see,' she said. She looked back down at her notepad.

He watched her transfer her focus back to her computer, eager to get back into professional mode, thinking she was in full control. So the date was his. First stage of the mission accomplished. If she wanted to think of it as some platonic outing then he was prepared to agree to it.

Agreeing to it didn't mean honouring it.

Winning the bet required getting her into his bed, not just taking her out. That would take time and effort and it was going to be interesting. He wasn't about to fail before he'd even begun.

'I'll pick you up tomorrow,' he said. 'Eleven-thirty. Let me know your address.'

She snapped her eyes back up.

'Eleven-thirty? In the morning?'

She looked wrong-footed, and he grinned.

'How long has it been—three years? You're obviously stuck in a rut of dinner-and-cinema.'

'But I thought we were going out for a drink.'

'We are,' he said, enjoying keeping her on her toes. 'Coffee. I'll see you tomorrow.'

CHAPTER THREE

ALICE FORD'S DATING SURVIVAL CRITERIA—
HOW TO IDENTIFY & AVOID A PLAYER.
Rule #1 First Date. How does he play it? A keeper will
be interested in getting to know you. A player will be
all about getting his hands on you.

ALICE HAD FORGOTTEN what a minefield it was just getting
ready for a first date, let alone actually going on one. Even
an experimental one for research purposes. Unfortunately
telling herself that dating him was a project, to be treated
in the same dispassionate way as a work assignment, didn't
seem to be having any effect on her nerves, which were
zipping around in her belly and making her knees wobbly.

Not that she actually gave a damn what Harry thought of
her or her appearance.

But still, it was ages since she'd been out and knowing
him they were bound to be going somewhere cutting-edge
trendy, probably for lunch. What the hell did the hip twenty-
something London crowd wear these days?

The imbalance in her wardrobe reflected the imbalance
in her life.

Still hanging in the cupboard: getting on for a dozen work
suits—some with trousers, some with skirts; a huge selection of shirts and blouses in sensible office styles; opaque

tights; court shoes; shoe boots, predominant colour scheme black, grey and blue.

Still in the drawer, although she felt like dragging them out and telling Harry to get stuffed, she was far too busy with a tub of ice cream and a box set to even think *of going out this side of Christmas:* a wide selection of greying lounge-wear track pants and vests, numerous pyjamas and bedsocks.

And finally, scattered over the bed, the contenders for today: a meagre selection of tops and well-worn T-shirts, a shirt in a soft pale grey material that she'd bought on impulse and never worn, a couple of pairs of jeans and a little black dress that was way too smart for daytime.

She'd started getting ready what felt like hours ago and suddenly there were five minutes left before he was due to show up and she still hadn't made a final decision on what to wear. She'd seriously underestimated the sheer size of the project of turning herself from hairy-legged couch potato into someone who might look at home hanging around a trendy London eatery. The hair removal alone had taken ages. Not that she intended to remove a single item of clothing in the presence of Harry Stephens, but it made her feel marginally more attractive knowing that if she did she wouldn't look like Bigfoot from the waist down.

All of which meant she'd now have to stick with the silver-grey shirt and jeans combo she was wearing and hope for the best.

She pushed her feet into black ballet flats and grabbed her black jacket just as the doorbell rang. Her stupid heart, which obviously was out of practice and working rustily at best, began hammering in her chest. For God's sake, Harry Stephens was not a boyfriend—he was a *task*. With any luck her body would quickly get to grips with that and revert to… well, to efficient-work-mode might actually be good.

He was right on time. She wondered if that was typical behaviour. Come across as perfect from the outset and your excuses might hold more weight when you start playing around in a few dates' time.

She took a deep breath and went for the door.

He was leaning against the jamb, wearing jeans and a dark blue shirt that picked out the colour of his eyes, a relaxed grin playing about his lips.

'Morning,' he said.

'Come in a sec, I just need to grab my bag.' She kept her voice as level as she could although her pulse rate was going crazy.

She was acutely aware of him as he followed her into the tiny sitting room. She could smell the light citrus of his aftershave on warm skin. She concentrated hard on staying calm.

'Nice place you've got,' he said, looking around. 'Very tidy.'

'Thanks,' she said.

'And interesting artwork.' He nodded at the wall above the fireplace and she glanced up.

'That's one of Tilly's pictures, my flatmate. She's quite arty.' She leaned over the back of the sofa to grab her bag. 'She's also out.'

'You look gorgeous,' he said as she turned back round, his blue gaze catching hers. He was closer behind her than she realised, close enough for her to see the dark flecks in his eyes, the light stubble defining his jawline. Her lack of heels meant she had to tilt her head up to meet his gaze.

Her stomach gave a slow and delicious flip. Keeping her mind on her plan even if her body wasn't, she put a quick couple of extra paces between them.

'Would you always say that as standard, or does it vary?' she asked, poised to mentally file away his answer.

'How do you mean?'

'Do you always compliment a woman when you take her out for the first time?'

He had a slightly bemused expression on his face.

'Yes,' he said. 'Always. Always tell her she looks fantastic.'

'Even if she doesn't?'

'Particularly if she doesn't. Not that I'd be going out with her if she looked like a moose. It's a no-brainer,' he said, grinning at her raised eyebrows. 'I want you to go out with me and have a good time, not slap me in the face.'

'So, technically, your compliment just now is meaningless because you would have given it even if I was dressed in a bin bag.'

A smile lifted the corner of his mouth and creased his eyes at the corners. He looked heartstoppingly gorgeous.

'What's so funny?'

'Nothing. I was just imagining you in a bin bag. Even more gorgeous than you look in those jeans.'

The predatory way he was looking at her made heat begin to curl through her stomach. The room was suddenly feeling too warm, too small with just the two of them in it.

'Let's just go,' she snapped.

She led the way outside and stared dismally down the path at his open-top sports car. Typical. All that time spent taming her hair into casually undone waves and by the time she'd done a journey in that it would have reverted to bird's nest.

Rule #2 Do not be seduced by compliments. A player will say anything to get what he wants.

Harry took the opportunity to catch his breath as she walked ahead of him down the steps. Whatever he'd expected, it wasn't this. He realised that without thinking he'd been waiting for her to open the door in her usual business suit.

She was unrecognisable as the tightly strung woman he encountered at work every day. Gone was the firmly coiled sleek hairdo in favour of dark waves that spilled over her shoulders, framing her face and highlighting the soft brown eyes and the high cheekbones. The absence of heels and harsh tailoring made her seem smaller and almost fragile.

All moisture had leeched unexpectedly from his mouth.

There was a soft vulnerability about her that she managed to smother with her relentlessly efficient business persona, keeping everyone at an arm's-length professional level. Seeing it now in the nervous dart of her eyes up to his made his senses zing into action.

He focused hard on starting the car, going through the automatic motions of pulling away into the late-morning traffic. Visual stimulation, that was all it was. Nothing more. Underneath the relaxed jeans and silvery shirt that emphasised her pale skin, she was exactly the same woman.

Higher maintenance.

The way she looked was irrelevant, in fact should simply be seen as a nice bonus. Winning was the aim here, and if he could have a good time along the way, so much the better. But still, he should be thinking how best to push her to the limit he needed, not being distracted by the delectable curve of her neck when she pushed her hair back.

Keep your eye on the prize.

He could sense her nerves from the way she held her bag on her lap, fiddled with its strap and looked straight ahead. He needed to get her to relax. Be as amenable and easy as possible until he could work out what made her tick.

She was just another woman, after all. How hard could it be?

'Where are we going, then?' she asked as he worked his way into central London. 'Some bar, I suppose, or restaurant.' He saw a flash of anxiety in the tense set of her jaw and knew he'd made the right decision by dismissing the cutting-edge trendy brasserie in Knightsbridge that had briefly crossed his mind. If anyone ever needed to loosen up a little, it was her.

'You'll see.'

'Regent's Park?'

He didn't miss the hint of cynicism in her voice as he led the way through the Clarence Gate entrance. It was a blue-skied September day and a broad pathway between perfectly manicured green lawns lay ahead of them in the glorious sunshine.

'When you said I needed to get out more, I didn't realise you meant it so literally,' Alice said.

'Now don't start grouching before we've even begun.' He grabbed her hand and tucked it through his arm, letting her step fall into line with his. 'You're going to love it. I thought we could go for a walk, maybe get a coffee, relax for a while, get to know each other. Then we can find somewhere for lunch. Where did you think I was taking you? Straight back to my shag-pad?'

'I wouldn't put anything past you.' She was glad of the sunshine warming her face, perfect for disguising a blush. 'I suppose I thought we'd go somewhere in town. A restaurant for lunch maybe. Trendier. Busier. With loads of background noise, music, people.'

'There are lots of places I could take you exactly like that. But I thought you might prefer something a bit more laid-back. Your whole life seems to revolve around work and when you do go out for dinner or drinks it's probably work-related too. When did you last take a walk in the park?'

'Back when I was living at home.' Her mind treated her to an unwelcome flash of the graffiti-festooned park near her mother's house in Dorset.

'You've lived in London all this time and you haven't been to the parks?'

She shook her head, bristling a little at the implication she was some kind of hermit.

'You don't seem a park kind of a person either,' she said defensively. He didn't.

'Well, that just goes to show how wrong you can be when you judge someone on second-hand information.'

She managed not to laugh at that. If he thought a curved ball of a daytime date would be enough to cast doubt on his playboy reputation, he was deluded.

'Sometimes a bit of open green space is just the thing. We can talk, get to know each other. Difficult to do that when you have to shout over music or elbow your way through crowds.'

Get to know each other. Her heart began to step up the beat, causing a rush of exasperation. *Why* couldn't she just block out all this physical-reaction claptrap and concentrate on the task at hand? As if she were interviewing a candidate for a job or handling a business meeting maybe.

She concentrated hard on the surroundings as they carried on strolling. The sun dappled the path through the trees and warmed her back.

'I can't believe you've been single for so long,' he was saying. 'You're smart, you're gorgeous. Why would someone like you stay out of the field so long? It just doesn't make sense.'

Her mind zeroed in. Flattery and compliments were obviously the order of the day on first dates with him, then. She wondered how long that would continue. Second date maybe? Or until he got you into his bed? She intended to abort her experiment way before it reached that point.

'I never really meant for it to be that long,' she said. 'I just got wrapped up in my professional life. You make me sound like some kind of an alien because I haven't done the London sights, but plenty of people put work first. There's nothing wrong with that.'

Landing a job at Innova had been a huge achievement for her. As a teenager she'd thrown herself head first into her schoolwork while her parents focused on tearing strips off one another, enjoying the escape it offered. Her excellent results had almost been a side-effect rather than the main aim. Not that she hadn't been delighted—it had enabled her to land the university place she'd wanted and then the job of her dreams.

'I never said there was.'

She took a sideways glance at him, walking beside her. He looked like an off-duty actor in his laid-back jeans and shirt and dark glasses, drawing glances from every girl that passed them. She felt bland and insignificant next to him with her old clothes and messy hair when she was used to dealing with him on the professional level playing field that was the office.

'You always get a good return on work,' she said, sticking grimly to a subject where she felt she could have the upper hand. He had the most slapdash work ethic she'd ever come across, which was all the more annoying because he undeniably got the job done. 'Doesn't matter how much effort you put in, it won't be wasted. It can only be beneficial.'

'Unlike your private life?'

'I didn't say that.'

'So you're quite happy with your work-life balance, then?'

Her standard answer, a resounding yes rehearsed to the point of perfection, lurked in her mouth.

'Not exactly,' she said, knowing he was watching her. 'I'll admit things may have got a bit one-sided.' She shrugged. 'Let's just say it's very easy to get used to nights in all the time. No pressure. No need to think about pleasing anyone else.'

And no worries about being hurt by anyone.

'And you get all the validation you want from achievements at work?'

'Exactly!' She looked up at him with a smile, pleased that he understood where she was coming from.

'Being successful doesn't have to come at the expense of a good time,' he said.

Well, of course, he would think that, wouldn't he?

'Spoken like an expert,' she said.

As they walked she began to find the city pace that was so ingrained being pushed back into a stroll by the surroundings. She took her jacket off and slung it over her arm. The lake came into view surrounded by trees and she could see pale blue wooden rowing boats out on the water along with ducks and geese. Only the occasional glimpse of buildings peeking through the trees belied the fact that this place was in the middle of the city. Tension in her shoulders, which was so perpetual she hadn't known it was there, slipped an unexpected notch.

They passed the empty bandstand and headed for a café, the grey-green wooden boat house next to the lake. Sunshine sparkled off the water.

She stood behind him as he bought coffees, trying not to notice the way he turned female heads. It was his height and broad shoulders that drew your first glance but the darkly handsome face that made you look twice. She was acutely aware of the interested and envious glances thrown her way as he turned to her, a takeaway coffee in each hand.

'Shall I grab a table?' she asked, scanning the terrace for a space.

He took a sip of his coffee and grinned at her.

'I've got a better idea.'

She looked up at him, squinting a little against the sunlight.

'What?'

Trepidation spiked a little as she wondered what the hell he might be suggesting. Finding a quiet spot among the trees for al-fresco sex maybe? Nothing would surprise her. She deliberately avoided taking his proffered hand, and followed him across the terrace and down the decking to the edge of the lake. As he took out his wallet and approached the attendant the penny finally dropped.

Not al-fresco sex, thank goodness, but still well outside her comfort zone.

She stopped in her tracks.

'You're hiring a rowing boat?'

She could hear the incredulity in her own voice.

He turned back to her, grinning.

'Yep.'

Despite her attempts to avoid him he grabbed her hand and tugged her gently along the decking towards the row of light blue wooden rowing boats.

She shook her head and tried to dig her heels into the decking, failing miserably in her ballet flats.

'I don't do boats.'

He gave an exasperated sigh.

'I'm hiring a rowing boat for an hour, not proposing we cross the Atlantic in a bathtub. Will you just relax for once and enjoy the fact that we are in London, it's a lovely sunny day and we are together? You want to get back into dating? The first thing you need to do is start loosening up or you'll get nowhere. Guys don't like high maintenance, you know. Not in the long term.'

'I am *not* high maintenance,' she snapped.

'Prove it, then,' he said, gesturing towards the boats.

She tried desperately to focus on her plan, her list, which

was the whole point of being here with him. Was she really going to back out at the first small hurdle, before she'd even had the chance to properly talk to him?

She gave an enormous exaggerated sigh and walked towards the boats.

The attendant was holding boat number twelve against the deck.

'Usual OK for you, sir?' he asked Harry. 'One hour, is it?'

She stopped in the ungainly act of straddling the water, one foot in the boat, one foot out of it, her coffee balanced in one hand and tote bag in the other, her ears suddenly on stalks.

The usual?

There she was thinking that at least he was imaginative, that the impromptu get-close-to-nature boat trip was actually quite thoughtful. But no.

Was this his date of choice to get a girl out of work mode and inject some fun? How many other girls had been treated to this supposedly spur-of-the-moment trip out?

Harry was all over the situation like a shot, rushing to gloss over the attendant's comment, clearly hoping she hadn't picked up on it.

'I'll take it from here, mate,' he cut in, grabbing the edge of the boat himself.

The usual.

It took a conscious effort not to shake her head in wonder. But she kept her mouth shut.

For now.

CHAPTER FOUR

*Rule #3 Be careful not to be seduced by dates that
are designed to impress but seem spur-of-the-moment.
Chances are it's been tried and tested with many girls
before you.*

IRRITABLY AWARE THAT she was wobbling all over the place,
Alice ignored Harry's hand and clambered into the boat on
her own. He leapt in and pushed away all in one graceful
fluid motion while she perched like a lunatic on the plank
seat at the end, clutching her tote bag against her chest in a
vice-grip. Realising what an uptight idiot she must look, she
slid her bag into the boat behind her and tried to sit back a
little without capsizing the stupid thing.

Harry manoeuvred the oars expertly as if he spent every
waking hour rowing girls around boating lakes. As if she
needed any further confirmation that this date was no one-
off. How many girls had sat in this boat with him in the past?
He really was the perfect candidate for player—she couldn't
have chosen better if she'd tried. This was all about what dating information she could gather, testing and fine-tuning the
list of rules she'd based on her past experience. And so far
he was delivering. In spades.

As they reached the middle of the lake he rested the oars
and let the boat bob gently, leaning down to pick up his coffee

from the bottom of the boat. The sun glinted off the water, warming her back gently. A couple of ducks swam past, and the peace and quiet was soothing.

'Not so bad, is it?' he said.

'It's lovely,' she admitted. Her life in the city revolved around concrete and crowds.

'See what you've been missing?'

'Yeah, well, if dating just meant having a good laugh and getting close to nature, maybe I wouldn't have taken the break.'

Harry watched her. Her hair rippled a little in the breeze as she looked down, picking lightly at the paint on the edge of the boat with her fingernail. What had happened to make someone like her—twenty-something, single, living in the most exciting city in the country—just opt out of a social life? He had her in a boat in the middle of a lake—she couldn't exactly run away from the subject if he pursued it.

'Why have you left it so long, then?' he asked. 'I mean, three years, that's some drought. What was it—were you cheated on?'

She didn't look up, but he saw her shoulders stiffen.

'Something like that.'

'Everyone has the odd bad experience. You shouldn't let it take your life over.'

'You'd know, of course,' she said, glancing up with a cynical smile. 'When it comes to the odd bad experience, you're an expert.'

He felt sudden irritation at the injustice of that comment. Not that he cared what she thought of him; it was the principle of it.

'I've never cheated on anyone. Not once.'

'Really?' she said, her sarcastic smile telling him she didn't believe a word.

'Like it or not, I'm honest. I make it clear from the start it's never going to be anything serious. Just like I did with you.'

'Get that in as early as possible so you can't be blamed when you throw in the towel?' she said, winking at him. 'Of course, you realise that when you say you don't want anything serious, women don't actually hear it.'

'Yes, they do. I make my intentions crystal clear.'

More so than ever since Ellie had opted for revenge instead of acceptance. Not that he was about to mention that to Alice. If she had the track record he thought she did, she was probably just a short step from bunny-boiler herself. Last thing he needed was to give her any ideas.

'OK, then,' she said. 'Maybe they *hear* what you're saying. But they don't *believe* it. You always think you can change him, that he won't be the same with you. It's like an inbuilt optimism women have.'

'So you think you can change me, then, do you?' he asked.

She held his gaze levelly, the brown eyes not remotely fazed. His pulse jumped.

'I fall into the exception category,' she said. 'If you have an extra reason for dating a man, then the optimism thing doesn't kick in. My reason for going out with you is to navigate the murky waters of dating again. You happen to be my guide.' She pointed an emphatic finger at him. 'It has nothing to do with wanting us to *actually* get together. It's a means to an end.'

'That doesn't preclude the fact that we could have a great time together.'

He deliberately held her gaze until she dropped her eyes. Sparring with her was actually turning out to be fun with her obstinate take on everything. She went back to picking at the paint, her pale skin taking on a golden hue in the sunlight. As he watched she tucked a stray wave of hair behind her ear, exposing the smooth softness of her neck. His eyes were drawn there.

'That's guaranteed, is it?' she said. 'Got your secret formula, a few tried and tested dates?' She gave up picking the paint and leaned back, tilting her head back a little and closing her eyes against the sunshine. 'I've got to hand it to you, I was really impressed.'

He shook his head lightly.

'How do you mean?'

She opened her eyes and looked at him.

'This,' she said, waving her hands around her to take in the park, the surroundings. 'I really liked the spontaneity of it. I thought you'd really given some thought to a date that might appeal to me. But you've done this one with loads of other girls, haven't you, this being your *usual* boat?'

She made sarcastic speech marks in the air with her fingers.

So she'd overheard the boat attendant. Damn. He'd thought he got away with that. And by the cynical look on her face, denial would be pointless.

'You got me,' he said.

'You certainly made it seem spur of the moment—you must have had plenty of practice. How many women have you rowed around this lake, Harry?' She held up a hand. 'Actually, don't answer that. I really don't care. For a second there I thought there was more to you than formulaic chat-up lines and by-rote dates.'

'Jealous?' he asked, just to see her reaction.

She laughed out loud. He grinned back.

'On the contrary, I'm pleased,' she said. 'You're giving me some fantastic insights into the kind of alarm-bell behaviour I should be looking for. Passing yourself off as bespoke and unpredictable when you've got a game plan going on in the background. That's how you snare them, is it?'

He felt a sudden flash of uncertainty. *Game plan.* As if she had some knowledge of his real motivation here. No more than a flash, though. There was no way she could know about the bet, and no way she would have agreed to date anyone if she knew such a thing existed.

He leaned forward and looked into the wide brown eyes, challenging the shrewd expression in them.

'None of that negates the fact that we're having a good time,' he said. 'Why analyse it any further than that when neither of us wants anything serious? We already agreed this is just going to be a few dates, some fun, so why not just let it be that? Come on, admit it. You've enjoyed it so far.'

She cut her eyes briefly away from his. Shrugged.

'Maybe.'

She took a sip of her coffee.

'OK, then,' he said. 'How about we focus on us? You and me. Without reference to anyone or anything that might have happened in the past. How about I agree to be straight with you right now about my intentions and then you can take it or leave it? Entirely up to you. Going into it eyes wide open. Ready?'

She looked at him with interest. A light frown-line touched her brow, and she tilted her chin upwards, making her look seriously cute.

'Go on then.'

'I think it's a shame that someone like you—young, single, no ties—is so buried in work that you never get out and have a good time. I want to change that. I want to learn what makes you tick. I think we can have fun together and, I can tell you right now, I intend to take you to bed.' He looked across the boat, right into her eyes. 'And when it stops being fun, I'll be happy to let it go. I can't be more up front than that, can I?' He wedged his coffee back on the floor of the boat and rested tanned forearms on the oars. 'If you want to bail out, just say so now. Although you might want to wait until I row us back.'

As Alice met his determined blue gaze her stomach did a soft and lazy flip. She kept her expression set, determined not to give the slightest indication that she felt as if she might dissolve into a hot puddle in the bottom of the boat. His arrogance was stunning. Then again, he had a constant stream of fawning women fanning his ego and letting him walk all over them.

She wondered how far he would go to pursue someone who didn't fall at his feet in the first half-hour. She was determined to show him she wasn't remotely beguiled by the charm.

'OK, then,' she said, making sure she held his gaze. 'As we're being up front. This is about getting out of the rut I seem to be in, *not* about hooking you. In actual fact you're pretty much irrelevant. It's the dating I'm interested in. I won't be booking up a wedding any time soon or crying in the toilets at work when it ends. Yes, I intend to have a good time, but you're up against a *CSI* box set, so don't flatter yourself that my standards are particularly high. And I have no intention of getting into bed with you any time soon.'

She sat back triumphantly.

He smiled at her then, a gorgeous smile with a hint of predator that made her heart rate speed up.

'I'll just have to work on changing your mind, then,' he said, keeping his eyes fixed on hers. 'Sounds like fun.'

Her zippy heartbeat showed no sign of slowing down. Deliberately ignoring it, she raised her coffee cup to him and grinned.

'Good luck with that.'

Harry began rowing again, slowly this time, heading further out to the middle of the lake.

'What were you like with your ex, then?' he asked her. 'Did you try to change him?'

She hadn't thought she'd needed to. In her mind Simon had been perfect. Right up until he betrayed her. No doubt Harry would have seen Simon's behaviour as nothing more than a laugh. They were cut from the same cloth.

'Come on,' he prompted when she didn't answer. 'You're happy to criticise the way I treat women. Don't give it if you can't take it. Haven't you ever wondered if your own behaviour might have contributed to the way you were treated in the past?'

She snapped her head up.

'What the hell is that supposed to mean?'

He shrugged.

'Well, have you always been this…' he struggled for the right words '…on the offensive?'

'On the offensive?'

'So tense and wound up about everything. Analysing every move a guy makes. I'm just making conversation, getting to know you. It's not easy when you're this…strung out.'

That was just about enough.

'I am *not* strung out!' she snarled, flinging her arms up, then gave an anguished squawk as the sudden movement made her tote bag overbalance. She made a too-late grab as it toppled over the side of the boat, taking with it her mobile phone, wallet and—most unthinkably of all—her personal organiser, bulging at the seams and stuffed with tickets, receipts and other vital paperwork and without which she simply could not function.

She scrambled frantically onto her knees as the boat rocked madly.

'What the hell are you doing?' Harry yelled, grabbing at the oars and struggling with them to calm the movement down.

'My bag!' she gabbled. 'It's fallen in.' She made a futile stretch for it as it bobbed out of reach, and gasped as cold water soaked her sleeves up to the elbow. 'My organiser!'

'Your *what*?'

'My organiser! My whole life is in there!' she shouted, incensed by his lack of concern. 'Don't just sit there!'

Getting up onto her knees, she leaned far over and paddled madly with her hands, making the boat rock all the more.

'For crying out loud, will you sit still?' he shouted.

Ignoring him, nothing mattering apart from the horror of bag, organiser, phone, purse, every facet of her life disappearing beneath the surface of the duck-infested lake, she scrambled to her feet and made a final lunge for the tote, gripping the side of the boat with one hand to hold herself in and realising a second too late that it was a stretch too far and the whole damn thing was going to capsize.

She was vaguely aware of a yell from Harry and a sudden *'whoosh!'* at the mass take-off of ducks and geese as the boat overturned, tipping both of them into freezing duck-poo-tainted water. An icy cold few seconds later and she surfaced with a gasping squeal, spluttering and coughing.

Harry surfaced a few feet away, gasping.

'Are you crazy?' he shouted at her, shaking water out of his hair. 'What the hell are you playing at?'

She thrashed wildly to keep her head above the surface. Swimming was surprisingly difficult when you were fully dressed and icy cold. Despite the lovely autumn day, the useless British sun had no water-warming ability whatsoever and she struggled for breath as she tried to concentrate on treading water instead of following the panicky impulse to flail her arms about.

And then he was there. She felt his arm slide firmly around her chest, then the solid muscle of his upper body worked to pull her one stroke at a time back towards the boat house, obviously the more sensible option since their boat was now drifting away upside down. She pulled herself together and tried to kick along with him.

By the time they reached the decking she was so cold she could hardly muster any energy to pull herself up and ended up being hauled out of the water like a beached whale by the extremely antagonistic boating attendant.

Harry climbed out next to her. She lay panting on her back, looking up at him. His shirt and jeans clung soaking wet to his body; his already dark hair was soaked to black. Drops of water clung to his eyelashes and he swiped water from his face with one hand.

'Still think you're not strung out?' he said.

The boat attendant had a face like thunder, muttering about vandals abusing the facilities and threatening to call security.

She hauled herself up onto her elbows indignantly.

'I'm not some teenager with an ASBO,' she said, through chattering teeth. 'It was an accident!'

Harry got to his feet and put a restraining hand on her shivering shoulder.

'You can't blame him. They probably get loads of drunken yobs messing about on the lake and mentioning your damned organiser isn't going to miraculously smooth things over. Let me handle it.'

He drew the man aside and disappeared with him inside the café.

Five minutes later and she was wrapped in a thermal foil blanket and slumped in a chair on the suntrap of a terrace. She discarded her squelchy ballet flats and tucked her cold feet underneath her, relishing the sun on her face and the sensation of feeling returning to her freezing extremities. If only the humiliation flushing through her could disappear that easily. People seated nearby were looking at her with interest.

Glancing down at herself, she realised with shock that her grey shirt was translucent when wet. Her pink lacy bra was clearly visible through it below the white goosebumpy skin of her décolletage. She snatched the foil blanket around her and held it tightly closed at the neck just as Harry, a foil blanket around his shoulders, crossed the terrace towards her with a steaming takeaway coffee in each hand.

'I'm really sorry,' she said, the moment he sat down. He put the coffee down in front of her. She waited for him to kick off, knowing she had no defence whatsoever, and trying to squash the rising panic at losing her bag, which was making a comeback now that the more immediate horror of public embarrassment and freezing to death was in decline. The bag was gone, and everything in it. There was no point in stressing about it now.

'If they manage to turn up any of our belongings they'll let me know,' he said.

'*Our* belongings?' She stared at him for a moment and suddenly realised what he meant with a rush of anguish. 'Your sunglasses! Oh, God, I'm so sorry. And what about your phone?'

He shook his head. 'Didn't have it with me. Just my wallet.' He shrugged good-naturedly. 'Money dries. There must have been something pretty damn mind-blowing in that bag to make you want to jump in after it,' he said. 'Life savings?'

She shook her head.

'My organiser,' she said.

He stared at her, eyebrows raised, and she sat back in her chair and put her head in her hands.

How could she tell him that keeping tabs on every aspect of her life was vital? Predictability was comforting. She'd had enough nasty surprises in the past to last her a lifetime, thanks very much. She peeked through her fingers and saw his questioning expression. 'You know, diary, appointments, that kind of thing.'

'You upended the boat because you couldn't be parted from your diary.'

Put like that it made her sound like a total control freak.

'I wouldn't expect you to understand. It probably wouldn't matter to you if you forgot a date or turned up late to a meeting.'

He jerked a thumb back towards the water.

'The bottom of the lake is the best place for that organiser. Think how liberating it is. Suddenly you're living in the moment. You can let life just happen to you instead of being controlled by all those appointments, all those obligations. Take it as it comes.'

Alice felt herself pale at the thought.

'Have you any idea how much my work success relies on me being organised?' she said. 'On my planning skills?'

He was watching her, the blue eyes shrewd.

'Don't you think that level of predictability is stifling?'

She frowned at him.

'No,' she said boldly. 'I don't.'

He looked at her questioningly, the ghost of a smile at the corners of his mouth, and she realised exactly how moronic that sounded.

A smile bubbled up before she could stop it and she shook her head in wonder at her own mad behaviour.

'OK, you might have had a point back there,' she said. 'Maybe I am a little strung out.'

He smiled back at her and her heart skipped a little at his understanding.

'I thought you'd be angry,' she said. 'I mean, look at you, what a nightmare. And your glasses. I'll pay for them, of course.'

She dreaded to think how much that would be; they'd obviously been designer. It was turning out to be an expensive day out.

'It doesn't matter,' he said. 'What's done is done. No point stressing about it now. I'll claim the sunglasses on insurance.'

He was so laid-back he was almost horizontal. She couldn't quite believe it. She kept waiting for his delayed anger to kick in. It didn't.

'For someone so irresponsible you're surprisingly good at taking responsibility,' she said.

He smiled a half smile at her. His hair was damply tousled, his blue eyes crinkling gently at the corners. Even soaked in stinky lake water he was gorgeous and her stomach gave a slow flip. Unfortunately she didn't need a mirror to know she must look a dripping frizzy-haired wreck. How unfair.

She felt oddly touched by his behaviour. Sewer-rat Simon hadn't thought twice about her feelings when he'd humiliated her in front of their friends. He'd laughed right along with them.

Today Harry had taken the embarrassment at full force right alongside her. He hadn't walked off and abandoned her to the anger of the park staff. He hadn't lost his temper with her, not that she would have blamed him. He'd done everything he could to dig them out of the situation. *Them*, not her. He'd treated them as a team, and afterwards had tried to make her feel she could dust herself down and chalk it up to experience.

Maybe he wasn't quite like her ex after all. She felt herself thaw towards him a tiny bit.

'Let's just say I've had some experience of smoothing over unruly teenage behaviour and it's stood me in good stead for this kind of situation,' he said.

'You mean you were an unruly teenager? Why am I not surprised?'

He'd probably led a life of irresponsibility since birth. No wonder nothing fazed him.

An odd little smile that she took to be nostalgic touched his lips.

'Something like that,' he said.

He stood up and held his hand out for her empty coffee cup. She couldn't shake the feeling that he was closing the subject. Of course he was. Heaven forbid that she actually find out something personal about him.

Rule #4 A player will not want to share in-depth personal details with you. If he tries to keep the conversation superficial and seems reluctant to talk about himself, chances are what he wants from you is superficial too.

'I was going to suggest lunch next,' he said. 'But under the circumstances maybe we'd better make our way back to the car. It's pretty hot in the sun now, should dry us off a bit more on the way.'

'Calling time on it before the first date's even over?' she said. 'Not that I could really blame you.'

She glanced down at herself and offered him a wry smile.

'I mean, look at me! Oven-ready turkey is *so* not a good look.'

In the soft sunlight her eyes were deep tawny, her damp hair softly tousled from the breeze across the lake. He caught a tantalising glimpse of pink lace underwear as she stood up before she managed to get the foil blanket clamped around her again and heat spiked in his abdomen. The loveliness of her was extremely necessary to counteract the infuriating insane high maintenance of her.

'I don't know,' he said. 'That look has merit—I was actually thinking I'd like to get you out of those wet clothes. But then that would be a bit of a leap ahead in the dating process.'

She laughed and blushed at the same time and his stomach flipped. He hadn't counted on her having a sense of humour. It was an unexpected discovery after the ice-cool exterior she kept in place at work.

'Do you really think I'd bail?' he said.

'You can't blame me for thinking you'd end it after one date,' she said, standing up. 'Especially after the way it's turned out. You have been known to do that, you know.'

'Only when it stops being fun.'

'And it's still fun? Despite my tipping us both in the lake?'

He grinned. The boating-lake date had a good track record for success, which was why he'd chosen it. If it went well he simply followed it up with dinner and then back to his place. Easy. No thought required.

For some bonkers reason, after what had happened today the repetitiveness of that process now felt dull. He had no idea what might happen next with her, and in spite of the soaking-wet clothes and the public stares, he found himself enjoying the expectation of that.

'It's still fun,' he said.

'What I don't understand is the appeal,' she said, looping her arm through his as they walked back through the park. His shoes squelched hideously as he steered her away from the shade and tried to walk her in the sunshine as much as possible.

'How do you mean?'

'Haven't you ever had a longer-than-five-minutes relationship? Don't you find all the chopping and changing exhausting?'

'No, I find it liberating.'

He glanced sideways at her for a moment, deciding whether to elaborate.

'In answer to your question, yes, I have had one or two longer relationships. Not much longer though, maybe a couple of months. Believe it or not I didn't really date much before I moved to London.'

'Where were you before?'

'Bath.'

'Girls there not good enough?' She tilted her head towards him and screwed her eyes up against the sun.

'No. I just had more on my plate back then. Since I moved here I only have to look out for myself. Why would I want to complicate things all over again?'

Right on cue his mind played the age-old flash of memory. His parents in the kitchen, at each other's throats as usual, and Susie creeping into his room to hide from the row, relying on him to make it go away, to look out for her. It hadn't been easy.

'Who else did you have to look out for?'

He shrugged the question off quickly. He certainly didn't need to be discussing the depths of his family life with her.

'Family ties,' he said vaguely. 'You know.'

'Not really. I don't have many of those.' She looked straight ahead. 'My family are all…'

He waited.

'Very independent.' She shrugged. 'Like I said before, I don't see much of them.'

He could tell by the throwaway comment followed by the bright smile that there was a lot more to it than that.

'So what's your success rate, then?' she asked him as he drove back to her house. 'With the boating-lake date.'

He grinned, not taking his eyes off the road.

'A hundred per cent.'

'Does that include me?'

'You're a work in progress. You don't count yet. But I'm

kind of working off-plan now. No one's made swimming part of the outing before.'

She laughed.

'At least I can't be accused of being boring.'

'No,' he said, glancing across at her and smiling his gorgeous smile. 'You certainly couldn't be accused of being that.'

Something in the depth of his voice caused a dizzying flip of anticipation in her stomach, followed up by crazy racing of her heart, and Tilly's comment from the other night flashed suddenly into her mind.

Just when would a guy like him go in for the first kiss?

Rule #5 First Kiss. A player will want to move things towards the physical as quickly as possible. Remember his main aim is not to get to know you but to get you into bed.

Harry was acutely aware of her next to him, the car feeling cosier this time because he'd closed the roof and put the heating on. Too damn cold having the wind pelt at you when you were wearing damp clothes. He could see by the way she was tautly upright, sitting forwards in her seat and staring through the windscreen that she was on edge. Just the way he wanted it. With his track record she'd be expecting him to leap on her like some predator, if not when he stopped the car then outside her front door. And let's face it, the usual Harry Stephens practice wouldn't be to make it to the door before he tested the water with a first kiss. Get it in right away and by the time you made it up the garden path you'd teased them into such a frenzy that you had a damn good chance of talking them into bed.

Which was the exact reason he wouldn't be doing any of those things.

The usual Harry Stephens practice wouldn't work on her. If he was going to get Alice into his bed, Alice with her player of an ex-boyfriend lurking in her past, he needed to prove there was more to him than a quick lay. He'd been doing pretty well on that front with his out-of-the-ordinary yet still intimate, carefully thoughtful choice of date, until the damn boat attendant had given him away. He needed to gain some ground back now, keep her guessing. And so acting to type wasn't an option. Plan of action: keep her hanging, then go all out to sweep her off her feet with the second date. By then, she'd be falling at his feet.

He wasn't about to let the behaviour of some guy in the depths of her past screw things up for him now.

Some guy like him.

No, he refused to accept that. His conscience was clear. She knew perfectly well this wasn't going to lead to hearts and butterflies, with the pair of them skipping off into the sunset. They both knew the only question between them was how far down the line it would go before one of them bailed; he just needed to make sure they made it to bed before that happened. The thought of reaching that point was slowly filling him with more and more anticipation as he got to know her, with her tightly wound attitude and the occasional glimpse of what fun she might be if she let her guard down. Unwinding her would be an experience to relish. And since she'd be expecting him to push things along as quickly as he could, now was his chance to buck her expectations and grab the upper hand.

Alice sat, hands bunched in her lap, stomach a squirming knot. She fixed her eyes on the road as he drove back to her house. On edge because she knew perfectly well what was coming next. She knew because she knew him. Her thoughts touched briefly on Arabella, one of many one-night stands.

She knew his modus operandi. Simon had been just the same. No qualms about moving things forwards quickly.

Somewhere between this car pulling up outside her terraced house and the short walk up the path to the front door, she could expect some move from him to kick them up to the next level. He would try to invite himself in for coffee—probable—or he might even go in for a kiss the moment he turned off the engine—toe-curlingly, spine-zingingly possible.

The bet crossed her mind, never far from the surface of her thoughts. She was aware that if he was involved in that she would be playing right into his hands by letting him kiss her.

But if she was to keep to her plans to observe his behaviour, she had to let this happen. And no putting a stop to it halfway through because London's most eligible bachelor might have money staked on getting her into bed. She still intended to end this whole thing before they got to that point—she could let this progress further without risking the stupid bet pool.

He didn't need to know that it meant nothing, that it was just part of an experiment, that it most certainly would never lead to sex.

The car turned into her road. She steeled herself mentally. She would experience this as a physical reaction only. No room for thought or emotion. This was all about coming up with a set of objective rules. Certainly not subjective, because she wasn't personally interested in him. She refused to acknowledge the tiny voice, deep down, telling her that part of her nerves had nothing to do with her project but simply came from the thought of what his mouth might feel like against hers after three kiss-free years.

As the car came to a standstill she curbed the sudden overwhelming desire to lick her lips, aware of his eyes on her as she turned to look at him.

The road was quiet. Lined with cars but no one around. Late afternoon. The shadows were long now, the sun dipping away behind the houses. He probably thought if he played this right they could spend the evening in bed and he wouldn't need to stay over. Genius. Her heart was pounding away and her stomach was doing cartwheels. And then she became gradually aware of the ongoing quiet burr of the engine. He hadn't turned it off, had just left it to tick over quietly.

He wasn't planning on leaving the car.

Which could only mean one thing: a kiss was on the cards. Right here, right now, in the car before he got out.

'Thanks,' she said. 'For driving me home.'

Anticipation had made her mouth dry so she felt as if she were speaking through a mouthful of dust.

'You're welcome,' he said, putting the car in gear.

For the first time her sweeping certainty slipped a notch. Might he actually be keen to get away?

As soon as the thought was out there it crystallised, and, no matter how hard she tried to squash the reaction, her mind insisted on immediately listing all the reasons why a sharp exit might actually appeal to him right now. Her meltdown in the middle of the boating lake, for example, behaviour he saw as 'strung out'—what a hideous term that was. She'd followed up his hot statement of intentions by tipping them into the freezing lake. Had he now decided she just wasn't worth the grief?

The reality of the situation kicked her firmly in the teeth with a whack of insecurity.

Harry, with his pick of London's women, who wasn't above having a one-night stand just because he could, didn't find her attractive enough even to go in for a first kiss. The anticipatory galloping of her heart slowed to a dragging-its-heels pace and the burn of embarrassment rose in her cheeks. If she wasn't alluring enough to snare someone like him, bearing in mind he already knew she didn't want anything serious, then it was no wonder she'd been an epic failure at keeping a man's interest and respect in the past. Hot on the heels of this thought came a boiling flush of anger at herself because she really shouldn't care whether he found her alluring or not.

'Goodbye, then,' she said, getting it in quickly before he could, taking control.

He gave her a chummy smile.

''Bye.'

She opened the car door, dimly aware of the uncomfortable way her jeans clung damply to her legs and the squish of her waterlogged shoes. She couldn't believe he hadn't made a move.

Alice climbed out and shut the door behind her. She paused to glance at him as she rounded the bonnet of the car and he gave her another friendly smile and a nod. He really was just going to drive away, then. No mention of a follow-up date. Nothing.

'Did you forget something?' The window glided smoothly down. He looked at her, eyebrows raised.

She realised she was standing in front of the car, staring at him through the windscreen and blocking his ability to go anywhere, and she pulled herself quickly together and walked onto the pavement, disbelief still coursing through her.

Her heart was thumping and a blush rose hotly in her cheeks. She should have walked smartly to the front door without looking back. Big mistake.

'No,' she lied.

'You're sure about that? Not waiting for something?'

The humiliation. He knew perfectly well what had been going through her mind and she stood back on the pavement, angry and flustered that he'd guessed her thoughts.

'You're actually going to just drive off? You're not going to try and wangle your way into my house for a *coffee*?'

She had years of entrenched dating etiquette and women's magazines on her side. A kiss at the end of a first date was practically an unwritten rule.

He shrugged.

'Nope.'

Her cheeks burned as he gave her a predatory grin that made her knees feel melty. He pressed a button and the window began to slide back up.

'You're really not going to kiss me?' she snapped at him through the closing gap.

'Maybe next time,' he said.

CHAPTER FIVE

Rule #6 How long before he calls? If he doesn't call or text you within twenty-four hours of your first date, you're not high on his priority list. He won't like committing to plans, so don't be surprised if he finishes a date without setting up the next one. He'll be keeping his schedule open in case something better comes along. A player will keep you hanging...

AN UNRESTFUL NIGHT later and Alice gave up on sleep around six and brewed mega-strength coffee. No word from him since he'd dropped her home the previous afternoon. Curiosity gnawed at her. What had he done with the evening? Had he gone out? Another date maybe? She had no clue if he wanted to see her again, yet she knew for a fact that a first date with Harry Stephens often meant second base, or even third.

He'd knocked her right back from first base yesterday.

At around eight o'clock Tilly's bedroom door slammed and a moment later she walked into the kitchen, face pale against her pillar-box hair, eyes bleary.

'It's Sunday morning. Are you insane?' she said, switching the kettle back on. 'What the hell are you doing up when you could be lying in?'

'I could ask you the same thing.'

'I've got a couple of parties today.'

Along with selling jewellery, Tilly had a face-painting business that she was growing via word-of-mouth at school gates.

'And since you are up, I really need a favour.'

'Go on,' Alice said, taking another mug from the cupboard for Tilly.

'Do you think you could cover for me for an hour or so this lunchtime? I've managed to double book so I've got two parties overlapping. I was going to leave the first one a bit early but that makes such a bad impression, and if you could set up at the second one I wouldn't have to.'

It wasn't as if she had a prior engagement.

'Go on, then, as it's just an hour.'

Tilly swiftly made them each a coffee.

'Now tell me why you're up at cockcrow,' she said, shoving a slice of bread in the toaster.

'My experiment is corrupted,' Alice said. 'He didn't kiss me. For some reason he didn't behave to type. King of the One-night Stand and he just drove off.' She covered her eyes briefly with her hand. 'It must be some kind of record. He beds anything with a pulse but he couldn't wait to get away from me.'

Overnight her insecurity had moved in and showed no sign of shifting, as if she had a very large, very ugly vulture sitting on her shoulder. She couldn't bear to tell Tilly she'd capsized the boat and made an idiot of them both in public. Harry had made her feel so much better about that the day before but he must have decided it wasn't an experience he fancied repeating.

She'd been so surprised by his support that its withdrawal smarted all the more.

She took a sip of her coffee.

'If I scare off a player like him, what the hell chance do I have of snaring someone decent? He hasn't called and there was no mention of a second date.'

Tilly picked up a piece of toast.

'At least now you know he's probably not got cash staked on landing you or he'd have done everything he could to get you straight into bed, right?'

That had crossed her mind. It didn't stop her picking at his motives in her head all the same.

'Whether or not he's in on the bet, it doesn't change who he is. Harry's face value is not thoughtful and considerate. It's full speed ahead.'

'Then perhaps he was tired. Or didn't feel well. Or had to visit his parents. There could be a hundred reasons that have nothing to do with you. Your whole ridiculous idea is flawed.'

Alice shook her head.

'No, it isn't. I thought about it overnight and I'm not giving up on my plan. I'm not going to wait for him to make a move and let him mess with my head. I'm going to take control. Maybe I can put him in a test situation that will show his real opinion of me.'

Even as she said the words an idea was forming in her mind.

'What kind of test situation?'

'You know, something he would never normally bother with. Some situation that he would find uncomfortable. If he runs a mile or tries to get out of it, well, then I'll know that he's just in it for what he can get. And you've just given me the perfect opportunity. I'll drag him along to help me this lunchtime with the kids. See how Mr Single with the buzzing social life handles doing something outside his comfort zone for a change.'

The idea of putting someone like Sewer-Rat Simon in an uncomfortable situation appealed. Let her be the driving force for a change. Men like Simon and Harry sat happily in their comfort zone. That was what being a player was all about. They called the shots. Not letting a woman have access to any part of their lives they didn't want them to, manipulating every situation to their advantage. This was her chance to take all that away and see how he fared.

She grabbed the house phone from the side table.

'What are you doing?' Tilly said.

'Taking control away from him,' she said, punching in numbers from memory. She felt hideously lost without her mobile. 'I should never have relinquished it in the first place, sitting in the car waiting for him to make a move like an idiot. I'm calling him.'

'Are you mad? Step away from the phone.'

'He hasn't made any reference to when he's going to see me again,' Alice said, not looking up. 'No phone call—he's just left me hanging. In any other situation I wouldn't mope around making a dash for the phone every time it rings. Why the hell should I? I'd clarify the situation myself. And that's just what I'm going to do right now.'

Tilly held out a hand and snapped her fingers for the phone.

'What?' Alice said, holding it out of reach.

'No good can possibly come of this. You called Simon after your first date with him and look how that ended up. You wait for him to call you, not the other way around. Do *not* call him.'

Alice flapped a shushing hand at her as she pressed a last button and clapped the phone to her ear. Tilly threw exasperated hands up and retreated to the kitchen.

After five or so rings she was resigned to the fact it would switch to voicemail so when he unexpectedly picked up her heartbeat zipped into speedy action.

'Hello?' His voice sounded a little slurry, as if she'd woken him up. Good.

'It's me,' she said deliberately, ears tuned to pick up the slightest floundering, whether he would recognise her immediately or hedge his bets in case it was another conquest.

'It's Sunday morning,' he said. A pause as if he was turning to look at a clock followed by a groan. 'For God's sake, it's just gone nine!'

'And?'

'We were together yesterday.'

So he did know instantly it was her. Perhaps she'd underestimated him. A tiny bit.

'And your point?'

'The whole idea of you dating me was to get you back out there—right? Well, you've got a long way to go if this is the way you normally behave. No wonder you've been walked over if you're this clingy.'

She felt a flash of defensive indignance.

'Clingy?'

'You ring guys the next morning?' he said. 'Not just the next morning but outrageously *early* the next morning. Do you have any idea what message that sends out?'

'Enthusiastic?' she said brightly.

'Needy,' he corrected.

Harry had thought the previous evening's holding off kissing her had been a stroke of genius that would intrigue her. Turned out it had. He just hadn't considered it might also feed her insecurity. Big time, by the sound of it. He felt a twinge in his gut, which might have been guilt at messing with her head. Then he remembered he hadn't had breakfast yet, it was obviously just hunger.

'It's been less than twenty-four hours,' he protested. With previous girlfriends, twenty-four hours would have been super-quick.

'How long would you leave it before ringing, then?' she

said. 'Come on, tell me how long is reasonable in your opinion?'

He paused. In some circumstances never was too soon. He groped for a length of time that wouldn't seem too outrageous.

'Couple of days maybe,' he said cautiously.

She made an exasperated noise.

'Seriously? If I wait for you to move things forward I could lose the will to live.'

'I thought you wouldn't want to rush things after so long on your own,' he protested.

'Exactly,' she said. 'It's been three years. Now I've made that decision I want to get on with it. So I thought I'd crack on and organise another date myself. That is, if you're up for it. Or was yesterday your way of telling me you want to bail?'

For a moment he was wrong-footed because his planned pull-out-all-the-stops second date was a sure-fire winner. Wining and dining at an exclusive high-rise restaurant with views over the city at night, followed by cocktails, followed by his place.

Then again, letting her have her head might be even more successful. What better way to impress her than to go along with what she wanted? He remembered her expectations the previous day—dating to her involved going out for a drink or the cinema. It screamed cliché. Tried and tested. How hard could that be?

'Oh, I'm up for it,' he said, wide awake now and thinking on his feet. 'At least if you organise it I can't be accused of using a formula. Over to you.'

'Great,' she said. 'I need to do a favour first for my flatmate. You can give me a hand with that and then maybe we can have lunch. Meet me at twelve. I'll get Tilly to text you the address.'

'Today?' he said. She wasn't wasting any time. 'Another daytime date?'

'Sounds like you were only planning on sleeping anyway,' she said. 'And didn't you know? Daytime dates are the new dinner-and-cinema.'

CHAPTER SIX

Rule #7 A player won't want to waste time when there's nothing in it for him. Set up a date that involves him doing something generous, something outside his comfort zone—and watch to see if he tries to wriggle out of it.

A LOVELY LEAFY street in Wimbledon. The address was for a large and beautiful three-storey house on the right. Balloons hung from the front door in pastel pink and white and a retro-style painted sign 'TO THE PARTY' pointed its arrow shape towards the wrought-iron-gated path at the side of the house.

Harry got out of the car, the word 'PARTY' flashing like a neon warning sign before his eyes. What the hell kind of favour were they meant to be doing for Tilly? He considered just calling Alice with an excuse, then realised he couldn't because as of yesterday she had no mobile phone. He locked the car and walked cautiously towards the house.

She appeared through the side gate as he approached.

'Great, you're on time,' she said, all smiles.

He stared at her aghast.

'Why on earth are you dressed as a fairy?'

'This?' she said, glancing down at herself as if she could have possibly forgotten she was wearing a floaty purple net dress and pink tights. Her hair was fastened up with some glittery ribbon and she had a pink flower painted on one cheek. She turned and led the way down the path. 'The costume adds to the fun of it, according to Tilly. And I'm all for being professional—even though I'm only doing her a favour I want to take it seriously. This is her own business, after all. She's built it up from scratch.'

He followed her, wondering in what universe being professional equated to wearing fancy dress. He felt as if he were in some surreal dream.

The path opened up into a huge garden behind the house, bathed in warm September sunshine. A close-cropped green lawn lined with beautifully manicured beds ran the length of it with trees offering shade at the end. Nestled in the corner was a painted wooden children's playhouse with a ladder. Pink and white bunting was draped along the hedges and between trees, fluttering lightly in the breeze. Double French doors at the back of the house opened onto a broad stone-flagged terrace. No sign of any other people. Alice led the way to the bottom of the garden where there was a cloth-covered trestle table and a couple of chairs, and began unpacking items from an enormous box.

'What exactly *is* Tilly's business?' he said, more on edge by the second.

When he'd seen the 'PARTY' sign he'd imagined waiting staff or maybe outside catering. Whoever owned the house was obviously minted and having a garden party. That would have been fine. He could hand round drinks and nibbles for an hour without any problem. Then with Alice indebted to him he could take her on for a lazy lunch somewhere— there were some gorgeous places in Wimbledon Village— and from there if he played his cards right the bet could be won before dark.

Alice shrugged.

'Party entertainment, I guess you'd call it. Face-painting,

party games, that kind of thing. She does children's birthdays or family parties where they get her in to occupy the kids while the adults mingle.' She laid out a row of coloured paints on the trestle table. 'Trouble is, she double-booked herself.'

She spoke with the disapproving air of someone whose life was so organised they never double-booked anything. Ever.

'She's finishing off at another party and she'll be here in an hour or so to take over. We just need to hold the fort for the first bit of it, as the kids arrive.'

She stood to one side and indicated the chair.

'Sit down, then, while I do your face.'

He stared at her in disbelief.

'Are you insane? I do not want my face painted.'

She totally ignored him.

'I'm not as good as Tilly, but I sometimes help her out and she gave me a crash course last year. I'm good enough to keep things ticking over until she gets here, but I could do with a warm up. Now, what would you like?'

She began counting off on her fingers.

'Puppy, monkey, tiger…'

'None of the above.'

He couldn't believe she was actually suggesting this.

She made an exasperated noise and plastered her hands on her net-skirted hips.

'You know, I really didn't take you for someone who doesn't have a sense of humour.'

'It isn't about having a sense of humour. It's just that when I do a party I like to be the one mingling with the grown-ups with a glass in my hand. I don't do family parties, I don't do fancy dress and I *especially* don't do kids. It's that simple.'

Gnawing his own arm off felt preferable right now to entertaining a gang of children. He'd more than done his stint of that in the past.

The bright smile faded, the expression on her face not

disappointed exactly, more resigned. As if this was exactly what she'd expected of him.

'Fine,' she said, trying to feign nonchalance. 'You can always bail. Just back out. I'll manage on my own.'

And from the tone in her voice he knew with a flash of clarity exactly what this was.

A test.

Her response to yesterday's discovery that the boating-lake date had been a little less than impromptu, followed by his admittedly deliberate refusal to kiss her. He'd put himself out there, told her she could choose what they'd do today, and she'd thrown this into the mix. He could jump ship; there was nothing making him stay here. Except he knew perfectly well that if he did, any chance of winning the bet would be over. And he would have let her get the better of him.

Definitely not acceptable. If anything it made him more determined than ever to have her.

He'd known all along that convincing her he didn't deserve his reputation was the way to win her over. And here was the opportunity to take a big step in that direction.

He sat grudgingly down in the chair.

'Can't you do something a bit tougher?' he grumbled. 'Spider-Man maybe?'

She stood in front of him and dabbed a brush in a pot of something on the table. He suddenly realised he was eye level with the soft creamy skin of her neck and décolletage as she leaned over him and he could smell the light scent of her perfume, something lemony and fresh. He settled back a little in the chair. Maybe there were compensations to the situation. He could quite happily look at that view for a while.

She tilted his chin upwards gently and he felt the light tickle of the brush as she stroked his cheek with it. This close he could see her with absolute clarity. The tiny scar that broke the smooth line of her upper lip, just to the right of the cupid's bow. That one little flaw seemed to highlight the full softness of her lips, painted lightly in a pale pink sparkly gloss, slightly parted. There was something so alluring about the way her tongue crept into the corner of her mouth as she concentrated on what she was doing. To look was to wonder how it would feel to take that delicious lower lip between his own. One gentle move and he could pull her into his lap on the chair and find out exactly how she tasted. Delicious heat began to pool low in his abdomen.

Like a bucket of cold water sloshing over him, all thoughts of passion disintegrated as the mingled shouts of excited children kicked in at the front of the house and built to a crescendo as they poured down the path.

'Finished,' she said, standing back and looking at him appraisingly. 'Perfect timing. It's all kicking off now.'

She grabbed a mirror from the table and held it in front of him with a grin.

'Pirate,' she said. 'You already had the stubble—it was just a matter of adding in a few scars and a bit of eyeliner. You might want to pop on an eyepatch or something—accessories are in that big box over there.'

He stared at his reflection in disbelief. What had she done to him? What might she do to him if he let her have free rein over this relationship?

He felt a sudden tug at his sleeve and tore his eyes away from his insane reflection to look down.

Small blonde girl with winning expression looking up at him.

He felt as if he were sailing back madly through time; the day was feeling crazier by the second. She looked just as Susie had when she was in her first decade—before her baby blonde hair took on its teenage light brown colour. He'd been in his mid-teens then. Straight home from school so she wouldn't be left home alone while their mother was goodness knew where.

He forced himself to smile down at her when what he wanted to do was exit the garden and never look back.

'Want your face painted?' he asked, glancing around for Alice. 'She does a very good fairy.'

Small blonde girl shook her head so fast her hair swished about.

'I want to be a pirate,' she said. 'Like you.'

Turned out painting faces was the easy part. Tilly had failed to mention the mayhem that a gang of under-tens could cause when faced with forming a queue.

'Wait your turn…wait your turn…' Alice chanted desperately, moving the glitter pot out of reach for the hundredth time. The adult party was now in full swing up on the terrace at the top of the garden, middle-class parents quaffing champagne and stuffing themselves with posh nibbles. She'd dispatched Harry up to the house to fetch a jug of water, where he was immediately hijacked by the yummy-mummy set. With hindsight, emphasising his resemblance to Johnny Depp by giving him a pirate twist had been a huge mistake. The next time she looked he was totally surrounded and she was the only one left in the place paying an iota of attention to the increasingly unruly small child contingent.

'Wait your *turn*!' she snapped.

The fairy outfit was itchy hot against her skin and she was rapidly losing her cool. What the hell had made this seem like a good idea? So preoccupied with putting Harry's interest in her to the test, she'd succeeded in plonking herself way outside her own comfort zone.

Harry elbowed his way through the throng of kids and put a jug of water down on the table alongside a flute of champagne.

'You didn't lose any time,' she snapped, nodding at the glass. 'You're meant to be helping out, not joining the party.'

He held a placating hand up.

'Chill out, will you? That glass is for you. They insisted. It would have been rude to refuse.'

She grabbed the flute and downed it in one as he looked on with a bemused expression on his face. Turning, she saw that three of the kids were now holding brushes and another was dabbling small fingers in the cerise paint pot and wiping them on the tablecloth.

'Right,' she said, trying to channel calm when she felt like standing on a chair and snarling at them all to go away. 'If you've finished chatting up the mums, maybe you can help me control the damn kids.'

He grinned at her.

'I thought you said it was just a matter of professionalism, getting them to form an organised queue…'

She turned in despair to watch the mayhem. Kids were now sifting through the accessories box, lobbing false beards, fright wigs and scarves through the air. Oblivious, the party carried on up on the terrace, the kids' unruly shouts drowned out by music and the sound of champagne corks popping.

'Yeah, well, I wasn't counting on the parents just taking a step back,' she said. 'I mean, what am I, a babysitter? No-o-o!' she squawked as the jug was knocked over and water spread across the table taking bright streaks of face paint with it. She frantically tried to mop up. 'I mean, any excuse to palm the kids off and party. When I have a family I'll be taking responsibility a *bit* more seriously. I mean, they're children, not pets.' She glanced around as the accessories box was finally upended. 'Although I've seen chimps that are better behaved.'

He watched her meltdown, vaguely amused smile playing about his lips, laid-back as ever.

'Finished?' he asked, when she paused for breath.

'Finished.'

'Right, then.' He put an arm around her shoulders and gave her a supportive squeeze. 'There's safety in numbers, right? United front. I'll keep them occupied, you tackle the mess, and then you can face-paint them one by one.'

Ten minutes later and her services were no longer the main attraction. He'd got a football from somewhere and it seemed playing a game with pirate Harry was much more fun than getting your face painted by the grumpy fairy. She watched the grin on his face as he passed the ball around and cheered them on, looking as if he was loving every minute just as much as the kids were. No one misbehaving now; it was more fun to play the game. Who would have thought it after his insistence that he had no interest in kids and no desire to spend time in a family atmosphere? Harry was a natural.

Standing on the sidelines was suddenly not enough. Why the hell was she trying to keep up some stupid professional impression when she could be joining in the fun? Dumping the brushes on the table, she kicked her shoes off and made a run for the ball.

The little blonde girl with the pirate face paint clamped the ball under one small arm and made a mad dash for the two fright wigs on the grass that represented a goal. As a couple of bigger boys moved in to tackle her, Alice swooped in, picked the girl up and ran with her and the ball at full pelt for the goal. She had it in her sights, was certain she was going to reach it when she too was tackled around the waist. She fell to the ground with a squeal. Small blonde girl made it over the line with the ball while Alice lay on her back on the soft grass, giggling uncontrollably. Harry lay next to her laughing, his arm still clamped around her.

'What the hell is this?'

Alice jumped and turned to see Tilly leaning over them, wearing a clown suit.

'Well, you two certainly look like you've got things under control,' she said, raising a false comedy eyebrow. 'Not. Maybe I should have left one of the kids in charge.'

Harry wiped face paint off while he waited for Alice to get changed. Ten minutes later she emerged from the house wearing jeans and a pink T-shirt. Tilly waved to them as they left the garden, a row of perfectly behaved children in front of her.

'See that?' Alice said. 'I don't know how she does it.'

'We were much more fun,' he said, slipping an arm around her shoulders and noticing that she didn't make a move to pull away. Maybe the past surreal hour had been worth it.

'Lunch?' he asked.

She nodded and smiled.

At a traditional-style pub in Wimbledon Village they found a cosy corner table and ordered baguettes and a joint side of fries.

His eyes were drawn to her face again and again. She'd taken the glitzy ribbon out of her hair and now it fell in soft waves to her shoulders. The only fairy evidence left were a few specks of glitter clinging to her lower lip, pulling his eyes in and inviting him to kiss them off. The image of her giggling next to him on the grass lingered in his mind. That funny, undone, enthusiastic girl was nothing like the starchy woman he knew from the office.

Of course he was just being sucked in because she was turning out to be such an off-the-wall foil to what had begun to feel like an endless cycle of predictable dating. He hadn't even realised he was in a rut until these last few days, but now he could see that his cut-to-the-chase game plan, storming in to get to first base as quickly as possible then ending the relationship before it really took hold, inevitably meant that things were always pretty superficial.

Using his cut-to-the-chase policy on Alice would have been an instant failure, so he'd been forced for a change to go softly-softly, get to know her, break down her defences. He hadn't really banked on any of that being such a laugh. He liked the way she threw herself into everything one hundred and ten per cent. Not enough for her to turn up and cover for Tilly in jeans and T-shirt, she'd gone for fancy dress. She'd joined in with the ball game with the same enthusiasm. In everything she went that step further than she needed to. He wondered with a rush of heat what that trait might mean when he finally took her to bed.

She took a sip of her drink.

'How did I do, then?' he asked.

'What do you mean?'

'That had to be some kind of payback for yesterday—right? I mean, please. Face-painting and a gang of kids?'

'If anyone got payback it was me,' she said. 'Those kids ran rings round me.'

'Ah, and did it put you off?'

'What?'

'Your ticking biological clock.'

So he hadn't forgotten her wailing meltdown at work last week.

She shook her head.

'No. Although based on today I might have to take parenting classes.'

He grinned. 'I don't know. I thought we made a crack team.'

'We did,' she said. 'You made up for my failings.'

'Rubbish. I just played good cop to your bad cop. Teamwork. That's the way it's meant to be with parenting.' He took a sip of his drink, thought twice about that comment. 'When it works right,' he added.

'I'll expect to see you settled down with a tribe of your own one day, then,' she said. 'When you eventually meet the right woman.' She pulled a sceptical face. 'Not that you'll know her when you do because you bail out almost as soon as you learn their name. The countdown to self-destruct pretty much starts the moment you ask them out, doesn't it?'

He toyed with his drink.

'Don't count on it.'

She sat back in her chair and looked at him, her eyes narrowed a little, as if she were trying to see inside him.

'I don't understand your aversion to kids. Not when something obviously comes so naturally to you. And you didn't exactly *look* like you hated every second of it.'

'It's different when they're not your own kids. You can walk away.'

'You make it sound like you've got a secret kid of your own stashed away somewhere.'

She said it with a jokey tone but she was looking at him intently.

'Don't be ridiculous.'

He spoke more sharply than he meant to and saw her recoil a little.

'Not exactly a kid of my own,' he said, not wanting to lose the ground he'd made with her. They'd made some kind of connection, a definite step forward. Giving her a bit of background could only take that further.

'Let's just say I have a good idea of what it's like to parent an under-ten. And I also know a bit about bailing out an unruly teen.'

She was watching him expectantly.

He shrugged.

'I've got a younger sister. I spent a lot of time looking out for her when she was small.'

He didn't make a habit of talking family. His life here in London was geared so much to living in the moment that he hadn't got to know anyone well enough to want to talk about his past. It was a novelty even to think back.

'When you say "looking out for her" you mean more than just the usual big-brother stuff? What about your mum and dad—weren't they around?'

The waitress appeared with their food and he waited until she left before speaking.

'My father left us when Susie was very young,' he said. 'I was about fourteen at the time.'

Alice sliced her baguette in half and added some fries to her plate. She was listening casually to him, grazing at her food, her easy interest encouraging him to go on.

'What about your mum?'

He sighed.

'She was there. Some of the time.'

He knew he was being cryptic. So many years of resentment of his mother made it seem unnatural to describe her in a positive way.

He took a deep breath.

'My mother suffers from mood swings. Dark periods where she's down to the point where she takes to her bed. Interspersed by other times where she pings to the other side of the spectrum and becomes the life and soul of the party, out every night. Sometimes she'd disappear for days.'

Her face was sympathetic.

'That kind of instability must be difficult for a small child. Was it a medical problem?'

'With hindsight I think it was—maybe it could have been controlled. But she would never admit to that, never see a doctor. Eventually my father met someone else and bailed.'

'What about you?'

'Susie is ten years younger than me. I ended up stepping in a lot with her. Taking her to school, picking her up, cooking for her, playing with her. Making sure she wasn't home alone.'

She was watching him, the expression in her eyes soft.

'You sound like a fantastic big brother.'

'I wasn't,' he said. He stared up at the ceiling briefly, the old pang of guilt smarting because that wasn't the way he would have had his life, given the choice. 'Please don't talk like that, like you're impressed. There were times when I resented Susie, really *blamed* her for being so damned needy. Like when I was in my late teens and she was about eight, being difficult, being stubborn. I was at home with her when I wanted to be out with my mates and hating every second of it. So don't think it was some unselfish act on my part. It wasn't. My father made a swift exit and I sometimes wished I had too.'

He glanced down in surprise as her hand crept unexpectedly across the table to touch his own.

'You still stayed though, didn't you?' she said. 'That's the point. Whether you were glad to or not, you took responsibility. You should be proud of that instead of feeling bad because maybe you would have liked things to pan out a different way.' She paused. 'We all have times in our lives when we wish for that.'

He took a long draught of his drink.

'Family ties,' he sighed. 'I decided a long time ago they weren't for me. I knew when Susie was old enough to manage by herself I'd be free. No one to rely on me or tie me down. Hold me back. The only person I have to worry about these days is me, and that's the way I want it.'

He picked at the fries on his plate, not really wanting them. She watched him in silence.

'What about you?' he asked.

'I don't really have family ties like that,' she said and took a bite of her baguette.

Funny how she'd always wanted them though. Wanted to be needed by her family, indispensable, never thinking of the flipside of it, the responsibility that Harry had experienced. But then she'd never had a sibling.

At least not one to stay for.

'My family are...' She searched for the right words. *A complete shambles* hovered on her lips.

'Very self-sufficient,' she said finally. 'I don't see much of them.'

'Do they live in London?'

'No,' she said. 'My father lives in Kent. My mother is near the south coast.'

'They split up?'

'When I was thirteen.' She smiled ruefully. 'I still saw them both, though. Not like you.'

She'd been passed between them like some commodity, not feeling wanted by either. It had felt as if they were arguing over who didn't have her, not over who did.

'I'm really sorry,' he said, meaning it.

She shook her head.

'Don't be. It was a long time ago and it was over pretty quickly. My parents never did any long-term thrashing out. My father just left at the first sign of trouble and my mother seemed glad to see the back of him. I never thought that was something to be grateful for at the time. At thirteen you just want them to stay together and keep trying. But in hindsight it was good that it didn't drag on. Neither of them was happy.'

'And are they happy now?'

Her mind flashed on her mother, a cougar with a taste for short-term flings, and twenty-something Alejandro, her most recent squeeze. The beauty of living away meant not being introduced to the hideous torrent of unsuitable men. At least her father was doing respectability, although why he couldn't have tried harder to do it with her and her mother she really didn't know.

She smiled brightly.

'My mother is a free spirit. She seems happy enough. My father very quickly found someone else, got married again, had another child.' Her mouth didn't even flinch as she added, 'A daughter.' She was long beyond the teenage feelings of being replaced because she wasn't somehow good enough. She was an adult now and she recognised those thoughts as childish. She'd built her own life instead where regard and respect were earned, not taken for granted, and where relationships were worked at.

He didn't leap in with a rush of sympathy and for that she was grateful.

'Even after all that, you still want a family of your own.'

She smiled at him.

'Absolutely. At least I know I can't make as bad a cock-up as they have.'

And the desire to belong with someone, to be a valued part of a family, had never left her.

'Of course, the beauty of the short-term no-strings fling is that you never reach the point of cock-up,' he said. 'You're not together long enough to hate one another or be cheated on.'

'But there has to come a point when short term isn't enough, doesn't there?'

'I don't see why. It works for me.' He raised his glass. 'To the short-term fling,' he said.

Alice clinked his glass with her own, shaking her head with an I-give-up smile on her lips. With his free hand he reached out and touched hers. Her pulse fluttered in response.

There was more to him than she'd guessed when she'd watched him pick up girls and put them down. Could she really blame him for not getting serious with that kind of child-hood behind him? It had obviously left him with a dislike of responsibility for others. This time now was his respite.

As they finished their meal and Harry paid the bill she realised she hadn't thought about her player-list for ages. Her experiment relied squarely on the premise that she didn't trust him and she wasn't about to let go of that. But for the first time it struck her that she might actually *like* him. Of course she was attracted to him, any woman in her right mind would be, but she hadn't realised they might have any common ground. In her head they had been poles apart. Now she found she liked the way he related to her, liked the way he seemed to wing it in life, and she could sympathise with his background. She knew better than anyone what it felt like to cope with upheaval in your teens.

As he pressed a hand to the small of her back, walking her out to his car, she ignored the zippy jolts it sent up her spine and fixed her mind back on her experiment, on keep-ing control. Liking him might be an option, but falling for him definitely wasn't.

As Harry pulled the car up outside her house all the feelings of nervous anticipation from their previous date recurred one by one. Fluttering stomach—*check*. Thundery heartbeat—*check*. Internal debate with self over whether he would kiss her—*check*.

OK, so she might have taken her eye off the ball a bit over lunch but only because she was thrown by the unexpected glimpse of his background. She was still under no illusions about the kind of character he was right now, in this moment. He was an avoid-at-all-costs player and it really shouldn't matter how or why he'd ended up that way.

Her hyped-up mind noted immediately that this time he switched off the engine. He turned to look at her, holding her gaze in his. Her heartbeat stepped up another notch and she wet her lips instinctively. How long had it been since she'd kissed a man? Three years? Longer? She wondered if that kind of ability had to be relearned or if you got straight back into it, like swimming or riding a bike.

'Thanks for lunch,' she said, because he'd insisted on picking up the tab again despite her protestations. She wondered if that policy might change if he got her into bed and clapped an instant lid on that thought.

He smiled, his eyes creasing gorgeously at the corners, and opened his door. 'I'll walk you to the door,' he said. 'And then of course I'll see you tomorrow at work.'

After what had happened the last time he dropped her home, this was a sure sign that he intended to play things differently now. Wasn't it? Filled with apprehension, she got out of the car too and walked down the path, aware of him close behind her.

At the door he was near enough for her to pick up the deep woody scent of his aftershave. The shadows were long, late afternoon giving way to evening now. Her stomach was a tight knot of tension. She had no clue if the next moment would have him walking away or closing the gap between them and the anticipation took her breath away.

'Are you going to kiss me this time?' she blurted out suddenly. 'Because if you're not, I'd rather skip all this small talk. I can do without all the angsty wondering if and when you're ever likely to call. Just get it over with and I can—'

He stopped her mid-sentence, leaning forward, catching the curve of her lips perfectly, deliciously with the gentlest, most featherlight touch. He took her lower lip between his own, sucked gently, making every sense in her body seem to zoom in on that one small connection, the touch of his lips and the gentle stroke of his thumb along her jaw. The knot of nerves in her belly loosened meltingly and seemed to slide downwards, pooling hotly at the top of her thighs.

Her sensible agenda was floundering somewhere at the edge of her consciousness. She slid her palms up over his chest, feeling every contour of the taut muscle through his thin T-shirt. She circled his neck, letting her fingers slide into his thick hair.

His free hand curled slowly around her waist, pulling her against him, moulding her body against his. She could feel the hard muscle of his thighs against hers and her knees felt suddenly elastic, as if they might fold underneath her if he carried on much longer.

And then he was slowly withdrawing from her, still with infinite gentleness, pausing to place a final baby kiss on her forehead before he turned to walk away down the path, back to his car. She watched him go, her heart thundering in her chest, surprise flooding in that he hadn't pressed things further. That would have been exactly her expectation—men like her ex, men like Harry, didn't do lingering kisses and slow respectful courting. They cut straight to the chase, kisses to be taken as far as they could go. In the past she'd gone along with it because she'd desperately wanted the relationship to work, to be real. At the expense of her own self-respect.

Harry's deliberate gentle slowness rocked the foundations of her experience of intimacy. In the depths of her mind she knew she wanted him all the more because he'd walked away. As her knees firmed up and she watched him drive away she felt the undeniable and totally disallowable skip of excitement in her chest.

She'd bucked his usual trend.

CHAPTER SEVEN

*Rule #8 A player will want to go public with his con-
quests. You are a trophy, not a girlfriend.*

THE BRINK OF a working week full of meetings to decide
the direction of the new account didn't really sit well with
a sleepless night.

Not one of this kind at least.

There had been many nights where sleep took a back seat,
of course. Sex into the small hours with no strings attached.
Yet that had never exhausted Harry's mind the way last night
had over one little kiss. That kiss was progress. A step towards the gravitas win that would show he had the perfect
touch. Cash and kudos would be in the bag.

He should have slept like a baby. Instead there were heated
delicious imaginings of how it might have been if he'd followed that kiss up instead of retreating to his car, of how the
softness of her skin might feel beneath his. Physical frustration wasn't the end of it. He hadn't accounted for the unexpected unease that she had given herself up to him. Not
completely. Not yet. But enough to push him towards this
frustrated sleepless state that felt innately wrong because
she had no idea of his hidden agenda.

Turned out he had a conscience. Or at least he seemed to
when it came to her. Who knew?

* * *

For the first time in months Alice wore her hair down for work and it was definitely not for the benefit of Harry Stephens. It was simply a part of her re-integration into socialising, an attempt to express a side of herself that wasn't totally work-driven.

And spending a little longer on her appearance this morning was sensible, because she was likely to be attracting some glances today from her work colleagues. She was actually looking forward to being the centre of attention for a change, this time for a good reason instead of a butt-of-the-joke reason. No one got a reputation like Harry's from being discreet. So she could expect him to be shouting from the rooftops today that he was dating Alice Ford.

In your face, betting ring participants.

He was late. Typical.

But she was prepared to overlook that as she emerged from the morning meeting expecting to be stared at with envy by the group of gossiping girls around the coffee machine and questioned about her new relationship by her extremely nosy PA. She'd planned to enjoy feeling smug for a bit, then maybe she would suggest to Harry that they grab a sandwich together at lunchtime. Just to cement the fact even further in the minds of her workmates.

Nothing.

No stares, no whispering, no nosy questions. No Harry. Eleven-thirty came and went and his desk remained empty. She kicked herself yet again for losing her mobile phone. The temptation to ring HR and see if he'd called in sick grew by the minute. She toyed with hacking into his work calendar. And the gnawing feeling that she was being played somehow wouldn't quit.

Worst of all, she really shouldn't be so infuriated. He was infiltrating her thoughts far too much. She should be completely detached and noting down this new behaviour in her notebook for proper unbiased analysis later.

She swept furiously into her twelve o'clock meeting because of course she really *felt* like discussing packaging right now, and there he suddenly was. As if he hadn't disappeared for half the day with no word. Two spaces along from her at the oval meeting-room table, a sheaf of notes in front of him. He caught her eye briefly and she shot what she hoped was a seriously dagger-filled look at him.

Harry raised eyebrows back at her. The frown knitting her eyebrows made her look seriously cute and he found it hard to keep his eyes from darting back to her. He'd left it as long as he could before coming in to work, scheduling in a morning meeting that he could have conducted by phone. All to put off what seemed inevitable. Her knotted-up attitude was bound to give them away. That was if she hadn't announced their relationship herself already.

He should be revelling in the ability to dangle his prize— so nearly in his grasp—in front of his colleagues, a large proportion of whom had money staked on nailing her themselves. Harry of a week or so ago would have really got off on that, without a moment's consideration for Alice, secure in the knowledge that they'd clearly agreed on it being just a bit of fun. He told himself it was simply because he wanted the bet won before he broadcast it. No sense in encouraging anyone else to hit on her.

But in the depths of his heart he knew his desire to keep her under wraps had nothing to do with outwitting the competition.

The whole idea felt vaguely seedy now. She wasn't some airhead who wouldn't care one way or the other. She was an intelligent woman and he found to his honest surprise that he wanted to be her friend. To hold her up like some almost-his trophy felt distasteful suddenly. There would be no enjoyment in it.

And so he pressed ahead with what he'd decided was his only option. Play down what had gone on between them. Getting a bit of professional distance in place ought to do it, possibly with some kind of disagreement. In short, putting her back up publicly so she would think twice about holding them up as some rainbows-and-butterflies couple.

A bit of antagonism ought to do the trick.

He waited until his input was required by the meeting, until all eyes were on him, and then he turned to Alice, keeping his voice neutral with a dash of animosity.

'Alice, have you had approval on the packaging design samples?' he snapped at her, knowing perfectly well that she hadn't—he'd spoken to the contact himself just that morning.

For a brief moment she stared at him, and then he saw the light blush creep upwards from the silk neckline of her blouse as she realised the CEO was watching her closely.

She flicked through her own sheaf of notes, and looked back at him with a 'what-the-hell-are-you-doing?' stare.

'I'm still waiting for a response on that,' she said.

He leapt straight back in.

'*If* you could chase,' he said irritably. 'We really can't move forward until that approval is pinned down. You're holding up the whole team.'

She was staring at him, lush mouth slightly open in furious disbelief at the obvious dig at her professional ability.

He swept on quickly to outlining his own proposals for brand development and the next time he took a glance at her she was staring down at her notes, a furious expression on her face.

Mission accomplished.

She practically rugby-tackled him by the water cooler outside the meeting room.

'What the hell was that all about?'

'What?'

'Treating me like some inefficient junior. Showing me up.'

He took a deliberate step backwards in case anyone saw them.

'I was being professional. That's more important than ever now that we're dating—if you're going to hang onto your respect with your colleagues we need to be whiter than white.'

For a moment she looked as if she might explode.

'Professionalism has never been a priority of yours before!' she snapped. 'So what the hell has changed?'

The CEO unexpectedly turned into the corridor flanked by a couple of cronies, just in time for her voice to hit crescendo pitch.

Harry grabbed her by the elbow and propelled her around the corner, out of sight and through the nearest door, which happened to be the stationery cupboard.

She was standing close, inches between them, her face upturned slightly to meet his in the dark stuffy space. He was hotly aware of her nearness. The musty smell of paper and print supplies mingled with the vanilla notes of her perfume. He could just make out the outline of her features and even in the dim light he could see she was furious. His mind chose that moment to play a rerun of yesterday's kiss and before he could stop himself he was sliding an arm around her waist.

She batted him away angrily.

'If you think I'm having some tryst with you in the damn stationery cupboard you're insane,' she snapped in a stage whisper. 'What the hell is the big deal with keeping our relationship under wraps? We're both professionals.' He saw her shrug in the semi-darkness. 'Well, I am...' she added as an afterthought.

'Why the hell are *you* so keen to broadcast it?' he hissed back. 'It doesn't make sense to me. We've agreed it's nothing serious, you're supposed to be Miss Professional, so you tell me how affairs with workmates fit into that.'

She made her voice slow and sarcastic. 'a) It isn't an affair, and b) in case you'd forgotten, I have a bit of a…what did you call it? *Reputation.* Aloof, you said, didn't you? Basically meaning frigid. Well, maybe dispelling the gossips might be nice for a change.'

That was so close to the premise of the bet that it made him feel suddenly cold inside. She knew how she was viewed and she hated it. What would she think if she knew he was playing on that very insecurity?

'I can't understand why you care so much about what other people might think of you,' he said. 'It's just gossip. I thought you were way stronger than that. Career driven, focused. I'm surprised you'd worry about that superficial rubbish.'

A long silence from her. Long enough for him to hope he'd got through to her.

'Maybe you have a point about the professionalism,' she said. 'Perhaps some distance at work would be sensible. I've not long had this promotion.'

'Exactly.'

He slid his arm back around her waist and tugged her closer.

'What are you doing?' she squeaked. 'How does this fit with keeping a professional distance?'

'I was talking about above the radar,' he said, lifting a hand to stroke her hair back from her cheek. Her skin felt satiny and heat began to climb through him. 'A bit of secrecy adds to the excitement. Now I've disrespected you in the boardroom, no one will suspect a thing. I could have you right here and no one would be any the wiser.'

He tangled his fingers in her hair and found her mouth with his in the semi-darkness.

The scent of aftershave, warm skin and the nearness of

him made Alice's knees feel as if they might buckle at any given moment. His lips tasted faintly of the strong coffee he liked. Heat tingled its way through her body. Rationality disappeared and she melted into the deliciousness of the moment, letting her hands tug his shirt free so she could slide them beneath it.

Sudden footsteps passed by on the other side of the door and brought her to her senses like a slap in the face, making her heart leap in her chest. She took an enormous step backwards, forgetting she was in the tiny room, and sat down with an ungainly thump on a stack of boxes. He looked down at her and even in the darkness she knew he was grinning.

'What if the CEO suddenly decides he needs an envelope?' she panted.

The very thought made her feel faint with panic. She could hear his breathing, fast, just like her own, and the thought that he was as fired up as she was made her stomach go soft. Then a chink of light slanted into the room as he opened the door a crack and glanced outside.

'Spoilsport,' he said as she got to her feet. 'There's no one out there. Where's your sense of adventure?'

'It's not about that,' she whispered, straightening her blouse. 'It's about being professional. I've got a reputation to think about.' She glanced his way with a mischievous grin. 'Whereas yours is already in tatters. I'm more than happy to announce to the team that we're dating like grown-ups, but being caught in a clinch with you in the stationery cupboard does *not* fit my managerial role.'

'Doesn't mean you don't want to!'

He leaned in and stole another quick soft kiss that made her heart thunder back into action, then gave in and held the door open for her.

As they walked together back down the hall she looked

straight ahead and kept a sensible distance between them, smiling and nodding efficiently at everyone who passed them.

'You won't need to worry for the next day or so anyway,' he said.

'How do you mean?'

'I'm away tonight. There's a development meeting at the client's head office tomorrow, focusing on the logo design. It's in Manchester.'

Manchester was two hundred miles away. A bit of distance, a chance to get some perspective. Exactly what she needed right now. She latched on to that thought and crushed the stupid sensation of disappointment that rose alongside it because she wouldn't see him for a day or so. For Pete's sake, she wasn't some lovesick teenager.

'Fine,' she said.

'Really?' He leaned in a little and she leaned the other way to compensate. 'Will you miss me?'

'Don't flatter yourself,' she said. 'I'll probably go out.'

'On your own?'

The question irked her. Did he actually think her social ability relied completely on him?

'I don't need to be on your arm to leave the house,' she said.

Harry slammed the door on the mini bar and flicked through the TV channels for the fifth time. He'd spent the early part of the evening eating dinner with colleagues and discussing the meeting tomorrow but for some reason the suggestion of going on for a drink elsewhere hadn't appealed in the way it usually did. He must be tired. Innova had stumped up for the usual basic standard of hotel and the room didn't have much to offer in terms of relaxation. He'd never noticed the mediocre standard of accommodation before—he was never in it for long enough to find anything to complain about.

He picked up the laminated TV instructions. For seven quid he could watch a choice of blockbuster, romantic comedy or porn. None of which appealed. He crushed the small insistent voice in his mind that he was missing her. He was just bored, that was all this was. It had absolutely nothing to do with the thought of Alice back in London. He really didn't care whether she actually *had* gone out alone or whether she'd just said that for effect. He was simply thinking of the bet. He didn't want her meeting anyone else now and scuppering his chances. Of winning the bet, of course, not of winning her.

In fact, just because he was away for the night, didn't mean he couldn't keep the pressure on and move things a bit further along from a distance.

Turning the TV off, he settled back on the bed, picked up his mobile and dialled Alice's home number.

Back to the old routine of box set, tea and biscuits and Kevin the cat snuggled up to her. Just as if her new foray into dating had never even happened. Surely it should feel like slipping back into a very comfortable pair of old slippers?

It felt like a bed of nails.

Why did she feel so damned antsy? So on edge? Alice Ford was now a slave to her so-called experimental relationship. Whoever the hell was in charge here, it wasn't her. And all because she'd allowed the project to get physical.

Only now, looking back, did she see how much her past relationships had been about sex. She'd wanted to believe they were about so much more—respect, love, the dream of long-term commitment. She'd convinced herself of that, putting all her trust in Simon. Yet in hindsight she could see how fast-moving it had all been. How she'd mistaken the fast physical intensity of it for love.

Simon wouldn't have passed up the chance to push last

night's kiss forward as far as it would go, ideally into the house and into bed. Their relationship had been full-on physical almost from the outset and now she knew that had been the whole point of it for Simon. In the face of that, the deliberate gentleness and then withdrawal of Harry yesterday, the obvious message being that this *wasn't* full speed ahead, was such a contrast to her expectations that it made her head spin.

And then there was today at work to think about. Her mind revisited it constantly, gnawed at it. She hadn't counted on things with Harry being such fun. She'd been so weighed down for the longest time by making an impression at work, furthering her career, that one day had drudgingly resembled the next for months now. Having him around meant she never knew what was coming and it made her feel edgy and alive. She liked feeling that way.

Was all this Harry's deliberate game plan aimed at gaining her trust? Was he playing it clever by going slow because he knew she'd been hurt in the past, or was there more to it than that? They'd made a real connection yesterday talking about family and she wanted to believe he felt that too. Yet to put her trust in him on the strength of gut feeling would be crazy.

Gut feeling was not reliable. She'd learned that the hard way.

The phone rang and she turned the volume down on the TV and casually picked it up. Probably one of Tilly's friends.

'Hello?'

'I thought you were going out and forging ahead with your new social life,' Harry said.

Her heartbeat kicked into action so quickly it almost felt as if she could hear it in her head. She sat back down on the sofa and took a calming sip of her tea.

'Bit of a long day today, so in the end I thought I'd have a night in,' she said, as if she had a massive circle of friends and hadn't spent the last three years right here on this sofa. 'How's Manchester?'

'Boring without you,' he said.

A flush of heat pulsed through her.

'Yeah right,' she said in a pull-the-other-one voice. It was already past ten-thirty; he'd clearly been out for the evening.

'Is that so hard to believe? I had dinner with the client earlier and I could have gone on to a club but instead I've come back to this excuse for a hotel room.'

'Bit tired, are you?'

He sighed.

'Why does everything have to have an ulterior motive with you? Is it so impossible to believe that I might just prefer getting to know you better to getting wasted out on the town?'

'Yes.'

He deepened his voice cheekily. 'What are you wearing?'

She removed the phone from her ear and stared at it in disbelief.

Phone sex? Really?

Why was she even surprised? He'd probably been out, failed to find a suitable one-night stand, and thought trying for long-distance sex with her might be worth a go. It was the perfect way for him to move things forward between them without taking the slightest risk. He probably thought he could talk her up into such a frenzy that she'd be gagging to sleep with him the moment he got back. She grinned to herself and put the phone back to her ear.

She'd soon see how keen he really was.

'Tartan pyjama bottoms, an old T-shirt and bunny slippers,' she said. 'I'm on the sofa with a cup of tea and the biscuit tin and I'm watching a box set with Kevin.'

'Kevin?'

'The cat.'

A pause. She wondered if he'd hung up. Or possibly fainted.

'Not what you were expecting?' she prompted.

'The usual kind of answer I get might be something a bit more silky. Or possibly even nothing.'

God, how tragic that these girls would say anything to please him.

'Sorry to disappoint you,' she said. 'I'm not your *usual* kind of girl.'

'No, you're definitely not that.'

She tried to fathom the meaning of that sentence from the tone of his voice but without seeing his expression it was impossible to know if he meant it in a good or bad way. She shook her head lightly to bring back some perspective because she really shouldn't care either way.

'If you think I'm about to have phone sex with you, you're sadly mistaken,' she said.

She was sure she could hear a smile in his voice.

'Shame. It could be such fun. And totally risk-free.'

Her stomach gave a slow and far-too-enjoyable flip. But nothing could induce her to put herself out there so openly with someone again.

'For all I know you could tape the call,' she said. 'I'm not about to have verbal sex when I could find myself turned into your ringtone.'

She'd learned from the past. Telephone calls could be taped. Photographs could be shared. Intimacy could be violated.

A stunned silence.

'You can't be serious.' His tone was utterly incredulous. 'I'd never do that. What do you take me for?'

'Really?'

He sounded shocked.

'I've never known anyone so paranoid. What the hell happened to you to make you think I'd be capable of that?'

'Careful, not paranoid,' she corrected. 'Your reputation
precedes you.'

'Could you give it a rest on my reputation?' he snapped
suddenly. 'I've told you before, I'm straight with people and
I never cheat. I just...don't like to get too involved.'

'And how long do you think you can carry on living like
that without burning out?'

'Living like what?'

'You act like a perpetual student, no sense of responsibility to others.'

'I'm just making the most of my freedom. No more, no
less. There's nothing wrong with that.'

'So back in Bath with your sister and your mum you were
deprived of all-night benders and one-night stands and you're
making up for it now, is that it?'

A pause.

'That's one way of looking at it.'

She thought she could hear caution in his voice, but she
warmed to her subject, taking a big mouthful of tea ready
to give him a piece of her mind.

'You feel like you're owed that kind of single social life
and you're damn well going to have it, regardless of whether
or not you're having a good time? That's just crazy.'

'I *am* having a good time. And I'm not the only one who's
distanced themselves from family. What about you?' he said,
turning the tables.

'That's different. Yes, my family are a nightmare. I try
to restrict my mother to small doses for the sake of my own
sanity. Her latest boyfriend is younger than me. And I'm just
not that close to my father. But not all of it was disastrous. Up
until I was about ten there were lots of good times. Seaside
holidays. We used to go to the coast and my dad would take

me crab fishing off the rocks at low tide. And we'd picnic on the beach. It's easy to just remember the bad stuff but there was a lot of good too. And at Christmas the whole family would get together, aunts, cousins, everyone.'

She felt a rush of sweet nostalgia as she remembered her childhood home crammed full of people.

'The whole thing collapsed because my parents had no staying power, no desire to work things out. They just threw in the towel on their relationship at the first sign of trouble. That's why disposable relationships aren't my thing. I won't make that mistake. I'm not afraid of commitment.'

She shoved away the nagging thought that perhaps her determination to hang grimly on to Simon and work at things had led to her coming off as a bit of a doormat. After all, she hadn't snatched the camera away from him, had she? Simon had argued that no one had *forced* her to pose for pictures. It was a thought she was used to pushing away. To acknowledge it would be to mess with blame and she'd spent the last three years apportioning that entirely to him.

'So you're not afraid to get serious, you're just afraid to take a chance on someone from the outset,' he pointed out.

'That's the drawback,' she said. 'I haven't really been a good judge of character when it comes to men. I'm trying to get past that now because I want the dream, whereas you've put the whole concept of family behind you without even trying. Tell me about *your* childhood. There must have been some good stuff.'

The memory of a holiday, way back in the depths of his past, flashed into Harry's mind.

'Way back, maybe,' he said. 'We went camping one time. When Susie was tiny and my father was still with us. I climbed every tree I could find and we cooked over a campfire.'

A weekend. Filed away so deeply he never referenced it

any more. His father had put an end to times like that. Had built them up and then knocked them down. And who was to say Harry was made of more committed stuff than that? She was right, families needed staying power and longevity and he hadn't exactly found that came easily to him so far. He couldn't risk becoming his father somewhere down the line, building up a happy family and then becoming suffocated by them and dropping them like a stone. Easier never to go there at all.

'There you go, then,' she said. 'Not all bad.'

'Not all. But enough.'

'What about Christmas? What do you do then?'

'I cook dinner. For Susie and my mother.'

This year he thought he might give that a miss too and stay put in London.

She failed to keep the surprise out of her voice.

'You can cook?'

'Again, your disbelief could be seen as insulting. Yep. Roast turkey, all the trimmings.'

'What else?'

'Stir-fries, curries, stews. Anything really.'

'From scratch?'

'You make me sound like a moron. Yes from scratch. What about you?'

'I do great sandwiches.'

'So we're perfect for each other. You can do the lunches, I'll do the dinners.'

This was more familiar ground. He let himself relax. They moved on from food to favourite films, TV shows, music. Bucket-list places they wanted to visit and things they wanted to do and try. His childhood ambition to be a famous cartoonist, hers to be Prime Minister.

Alice's DVD had long since finished. As she finally put the phone down it occurred to her that her eyes felt scratchy with lack of sleep and she was getting cold. She realised that the central heating had clicked off ages ago.

Time had somehow slipped under her radar while they talked, as if he'd captured her attention so completely that it had become irrelevant. She became aware that the quality of the light in the room was different. Almost imperceptibly, dawn was filtering in through the curtains and Kevin was changing from sleepy couch potato in the small of her back to morning-alert.

They'd ended up chatting for hours. Where the hell had the night gone? And what the hell was she doing?

However she looked at it, she'd gone way beyond the necessity of her project. Dating Harry was becoming less about being a task and more about enjoying herself. And she really wasn't sure how she felt about that.

Tired from the all-night phone call, Harry worked his way through the morning's meeting with what felt like cotton-wool in his brain, fighting the constant return of his thoughts to Alice. Tiredness was all it was, he insisted to himself. A good night's sleep in his own bed and he'd be ready to face her at the office on his usual detached terms.

It was still lunchtime at Innova when Harry got back to the office and he looked around for Alice, thinking maybe he could take her somewhere for coffee and a sandwich. He was a bit concerned at how much pleasure that thought gave him.

He checked the kitchen, thinking she might be there, and didn't make it out again.

Alice stashed her meeting notes on her desk and went to grab her yogurt and banana from the fridge. She glanced at Harry's empty desk as she passed, a tight knot of nerves in the pit of her stomach. Still no sign of him returning from Manchester. And then as if on cue she rounded the corner and saw him across the office, standing in the doorway of the tiny staff kitchen. Her stomach gave a gigantic leap in response that faded to a damp squib of a flutter as she took in the scene.

He was wearing a beautifully cut dark blue suit and a blonde woman.

Her heart performed an unexpected lurch as she did a double-take. He wore the suit in his usual laconic style— top button undone and tie loosened—and, whoever she was, she was holding the lapel of his jacket in an urgent grip and talking earnestly to him.

Alice's shocked eyes slowly processed the details as she walked closer. Was he cheating on her? She was stunned by the wave of disappointment in that thought. After talking to him for hours, getting to know him, she'd actually begun to question all her prejudices about him. As she got closer she vaguely recognised the girl as one of the marketing assistants. Harry's hands were in his pockets and he was shaking his head.

'I've been thinking,' the girl was saying, her upturned face imploring and her attention entirely focused on Harry. 'I can see now I was pushing things along too quickly, and that's so not what I wanted.'

'Right,' Harry said. She saw him try to take a step back but the woman had his jacket in a vice-grip. He glanced up and jumped visibly as he caught sight of Alice next to the photocopier. *Guilty conscience?* She raised her eyebrows and gave him a smile, injecting as much sarcasm into it as she could muster.

'Zoe, that's very sweet but it's been over between us for ages,' Harry said, rolling his eyes at Alice in a 'can-you-be-lieve-this' gesture. 'It was fun while it lasted but it was never going to be anything serious.'

Yet another of his dropped-like-a-stone exes. She'd been

knocked off-task by the night spent chatting to him. Well, here it was: her wake-up call. *This* was how Harry treated women. He took what he wanted and then chucked them away.

'I know I was too full-on but things are different now. And I'm sorry I was so angry when you ended it. I don't want to change you, or pressure you.' Zoe's face was turned imploringly up to his. For her, Alice didn't exist. 'I bought you an iced coffee from the café round the corner,' she said, nodding at a couple of cups on a nearby desk. 'I thought we could have a quiet talk in the staff room. Peace offering— what do you say?'

Alice stared at the girl in disbelief. Was she for real? Did she have no self-respect at all?

Her mind tried to sideslip back to a time when she'd regarded Simon in exactly the same way—apologising for being too clingy, excusing his bad behaviour by blaming it on herself. She crushed the memory hard. She would not be that stupid downtrodden girl any more.

'Please?' Zoe said.

Simon. Harry. In that moment they blended into one. Alice walked as if in a dream over to the table and picked up one of the plastic cups. It was icy cold beneath her fingers as she peeled off the lid. She took a couple of quick strides, reached up and tipped the whole thing in one freezing splash over Harry's head. Ice cubes clattered to the floor around his feet and brown liquid dripped down over his face and neck as he gasped at the sudden cold.

Zoe leapt back as if burned.

'Why the hell did you do that?' she squawked at Alice, horrified.

Alice tossed the empty cup in a nearby bin and rubbed her sticky fingers together.

'Because unlike half the office, I don't have *mug* written on my forehead when it comes to him. He deserves it.'

She was vaguely aware of Harry in the background wiping coffee from his face and licking his fingers and, she was surprised to see, grinning in spite of the mess.

She patted Zoe comfortingly on the shoulder as she walked away.

'You'll thank me for that one day,' she said.

CHAPTER EIGHT

'I KNOW WE agreed to keep things quiet between us at work but you didn't have to go quite that far for a cover story,' Harry said, running a hand through his hair.

A rinse under the tap in the men's room hadn't quite removed the stickiness from his hair. He'd abandoned his jacket and mopped the worst of the coffee splashes from his shirt. As a result he'd had no time to eat lunch and only managed to catch up with Alice in the lift at the end of the day.

The situation with Zoe should have been nothing more than an amusing inconvenience to him. Strangely there hadn't been the usual temptation that might accompany such a conversation with an ex-conquest—she'd practically offered herself on a plate and he couldn't have been less interested. Taking her out again would only make things worse. Maybe his recent brush with revenge had affected him more deeply than he thought.

'Oh, so you think it was all about me watching your back and putting people off the scent?'

She gave a cynical laugh and pressed the button for the ground floor. The lift shuddered into life.

He held her gaze, noticing that she didn't drop her eyes. Instead she looked at him with confidence.

'Wasn't it?'

'Of course not. It was about respect. That poor deluded girl.'

He opened his mouth to protest and she talked right over him.

'Don't kick in with all that claptrap about how you're up front with them and you never make promises. However you dress it up, you basically sleep with these girls and then dump them. You're kidding yourself if you think you're treating them fairly. For most women sex isn't something you do lightly. Don't you understand what that might do to their self-esteem—that the moment you've got that from them you lose interest?'

He looked at her, all fired up and indignant, and heat sparked in his abdomen. The tiny frown-line knitting her eyebrows made her look delectable. He could have Zoe back in his bed with one simple phone call, yet he had no idea what he would need to do to get Alice there. The challenge of that was just tantalising.

She looked down at the box file in her arms for a moment.

'I'm not sure where gunking you in iced coffee came from,' she said, shaking her head wonderingly. 'It just seemed like a good idea at the time.' She glanced up at him with a little half smile that touched his heart. 'Maybe I over-reacted.' She paused. 'A little bit.'

'Don't,' he said.

'What?'

'Don't backtrack. You said what you thought. Maybe part of the problem is that girls don't do that enough. It's all so easy to just do what you want when someone tells you what you want to hear, whether or not you think it's right or wrong.'

'When you put it like that it isn't much of a step away from bullying,' she said. 'I'm not backtracking. You so deserved the gunking!'

Her tone of voice was jokey and she was grinning mischievously at him, but the comment hit him like a sledgehammer nonetheless. Was that really what she thought of him? Why did he even care?

The lift pinged to a standstill and as the doors opened she walked full speed ahead out into the ground-floor reception hall.

'Maybe a *frappé* in the face was a wake-up call I could do with,' he called after her.

She stopped and waited. He caught her up by the doors.

'Really?' she said, eyebrows raised, a light smile touching the corners of her mouth.

'It's easy to go too far, trample on people's feelings, when they act like a pushover.'

'I always thought that was exactly what did it for you—someone who will go along with whatever you want in the name of fun.'

'Maybe it was. And maybe you're right and I should think about consequences more.'

Especially as all the consequences he'd encountered recently had been unpleasant ones. It wasn't just today. There was the whole revenge mess Ellie had unleashed on him, making him wonder if a few dates' worth of single fun was worth all the grief.

And deep down, deny it though he might, there was this new feeling that women per se were no longer particularly interesting. All thoughts seemed to be consumed by Alice, and she was hardly about to leap into bed and put him out of his misery.

She shifted the box file from one arm to the other and looked at him with narrowed eyes.

'Is that some kind of apology? To womankind at large?'

He shrugged.

'Am I forgiven if it is? Still up for going out tomorrow?'

For some reason her answer seemed massively important to him.

She nodded and he felt a happy flash of relief, which was totally uncharacteristic. He really was getting sucked in by his refusal to lose; all his perspective had gone out of the window.

'There's a work party in town,' she said. 'Roger from Accounts is leaving. Maybe we could go to that.'

His heart sank. Keeping his pursuit of her under wraps out of work time wasn't likely to be easy. But he would have agreed to anything.

'I'll pick you up at eight,' he said, leaning in to kiss her cheek.

She grimaced.

'You might want to shower a few times before then. You absolutely reek of cheap sugary coffee.'

Harry kept the taxi waiting outside and rang the doorbell, the unease in his stomach seething there. He really should have seen this coming. Of course she'd want to flex her new dating muscles by going out with work. And shouldn't he really be pleased with that?

But he'd spent these past days getting to know her without sex on the agenda. And as the time passed the bet felt more and more like a hideous liability than a laugh.

She opened the door and agitation spiralled off the radar.

Her wide brown eyes were highlighted by some smudgy dark make-up that emphasised the soft porcelain of her complexion. She wore her dark hair long, its waves curling softly to the creamy skin of her collarbones, exposed deliciously by the boat neck of the black dress she wore. It fell in a softly flowing skirt of layered chiffon, which ended an inch or so above her knees. All those trouser suits and opaque tights at the office meant he'd never noticed she even had legs, let alone tapered slender ones like that. His tongue felt as if it were melded to the roof of his mouth.

'You look beautiful,' he managed, swallowing hard.

She gave a here-we-go-again roll of her eyes.

'I toyed with the idea of wearing a bin bag, just to see if I got that stock reply,' she said, reaching behind the door to grab her bag from the side table. She made a move to walk past him out of the door, his compliment instantly dismissed as worthless. He regretted his flip manner on that first date now.

'Alice,' he said.

She glanced back at him as she shrugged her jacket on.

'I mean it. You look beautiful. Far too good for some dull work party. Why don't I take you somewhere else? For dinner maybe?'

She was looking at him, eyes narrowed.

'Don't be daft. I've been looking forward to this. Do you realise I've worked for Innova for four years and I've only been out for a drink with work half a dozen times, all of them in the first month or so when I was trying to settle in? I haven't even done a Christmas party yet. Oh, I do business lunches, that kind of thing. But they're work really, not play. I got myself into such a damn rut.'

He didn't answer and she looked up at him then with an odd little smile and disappointment in her eyes that brought a fresh wave of guilt.

'I thought you went to all these things. What's the big deal?' She frowned. 'I suppose I could make my own way there if you're not up for it.'

The thought of her turning up among the pack of wolves he worked with, looking like that with her suddenly open attitude, filled him with horror. Even without the bet incentive any man in his right mind would be blown away by her.

'No, it's fine,' he backtracked. 'Just a suggestion.'

She slammed her front door shut and walked towards the waiting taxi. He followed her down the path, disquiet churning in his gut.

He knew perfectly well that one stray comment could give the game away tonight and let her know he was only dating her for a bet. Suddenly he couldn't care less about a few hundred quid and a bit of glory over his mates. All he could think was how it would make her feel if she found out this was all some stupid game. She would be hurt. Their friendship, whatever else this was between them, would be over.

What the hell should that matter? Even if there was no bet it would be over between them anyway in a week or so, was always going to be. That thought made his mood plummet and it dawned on him in that moment with a sudden flash of clarity.

He was in too deep.

The party was at exactly the kind of bar in West London that she imagined Harry spent every ounce of his spare time in, on the prowl. Already buzzing with people, it had a lively and sophisticated atmosphere. There was a long backlit bar and subtle scarlet-tinged lighting picked out the tables, one of them occupied by the usual suspects from work. A couple of weeks ago there was no way she would have contemplated coming here and, despite what she'd said to Harry, if he hadn't accompanied her she would never have made her way here by herself. Maybe in another month or so when she'd finished her study of Harry, she'd be ready by then, fully prepped to weed out the dross and find herself a keeper. The bet might have knocked her confidence but at least it had pushed her to take stock of herself. At least she had that. She was gradually coming out of her antisocial shell.

Arriving with Harry was very different from walking in alone. He was the centre of attention at once and she was the subject of curious and definitely envious glances. She was aware of his hand pressed lightly at the small of her back, glad of it. Yet in the few short minutes since he'd left her to buy drinks she turned in her seat to see him surrounded by women and looking as if he was enjoying every second. Her eyes widened when he pulled up a stool as if he was settling in for the evening. The damn cheek of it! He was meant to be her date.

The red-haired girl who'd recently joined the company smiled up at him. Skin-tight trousers under a floating silk top and killer heels. Her red hair fell almost to the middle of her back. With his dark good looks picked out in the mirrored lighting of the bar, Harry looked perfectly suited to her. The pair of them looked as if they were in some TV ad for a cutting-edge new drink.

He hadn't so much as glanced Alice's way and it was a sharp reminder of his awful reputation. You didn't get a reputation like that by magic—you *earned* it. By behaving in the way he was right now.

Self-consciousness kicked in as if it had never really been away. She felt out of place. And of course she was. Her place was at home on the sofa, not out with the crowd. She toyed with the idea of making a quick exit to the Ladies to take stock and decide what to do.

That's just about enough.

Something snapped inside her and as boiling humiliation began to rise she forced it back down. She wasn't about to let him play her like this. Exit to the Ladies? She could do better than that. She hadn't spent hours observing him for nothing. Playing him at his own game should be a piece of cake.

Compliments—that was how he started out, wasn't it?

She turned to John, one of the Design team, flashed him her most brilliant smile and rested her hand lightly on his arm.

'I've got to tell you, I thought your new logo ideas were

completely *fabulous*,' she gushed, although privately she'd thought a toddler with a wax crayon could have come up with them. 'Genius.'

John beamed at her and immediately grabbed the opportunity to bury her in a ton more of his suggestions. She tried to make her eyes focus on him when they wanted to glaze over. And then a sidelong glance gave her a burst of triumph. Harry was suddenly ignoring his gaggle of women and was staring over at her, a look on his face that could only be described as furious. Hah! Result!

Harry tried and failed to tune out the overenthusiastic babble of Saskia, the new addition to the secretarial team. He could tell by her body language, by the way she hung on every word he said, that with a few well-placed lines he could hook her. He found he had absolutely no interest in doing so.

Unheard of.

He was unable to tear his gaze away from Alice as she spoke animatedly to the rest of the table. He could see the men at the table hanging on her every word and John from his own team actually had the gall to rest his arm along the back of her chair.

Does that oaf have a stake in the bet ring?

If John didn't have a stake he was no threat, right?

Wrong.

Suddenly the bet seemed utterly unimportant. As he watched Alice laughed at something John said and the fiery stab of jealousy he felt in response told him in a way he couldn't deny that he had a lot more at stake here than just money.

He was off the stool before he really knew what he intended to do. Maybe cross to the table and join them while crushing the urge to knock John's head from his shoulders.

He didn't make as much as a step away from the bar. Last seen gloating after shredding his wardrobe and trashing his laptop, his ex-girlfriend Ellie elbowed her way unexpectedly into the middle of the group, which until then had consisted of himself and four eligible women. She had a glass of red wine in one hand and a look on her face that told him if he thought she'd got the anger out of her system, he was deluded.

Great.

'Don't get too keen, girls,' she announced, her eyes fixed on Harry. 'There are a few things you should know up front about Mr Perfect before you go any further.'

Oh, for God's sake. Just what he needed after spending so much effort convincing Alice he didn't deserve his awful reputation: an angry scene with a jilted ex.

'You think that gorgeous dark hair's natural?' Ellie glanced around at the speechless girls as she waved a hand towards Harry's head. 'Wait and see what's underneath the Just For Men hair dye.'

Harry stared at the aghast faces.

'You wonder how anyone can actually *be* that gorgeous?' she asked, warming to her subject. 'Well, truth is, he's not. It's all fake. And he'll dump you the moment he beds you. That extreme sports tan? Fake. And he waxes.' She raised her voice to a shout above the bar's background music. 'Three words, Harry. Back, sack and crack!'

Harry choked on his drink. Enough was enough. He slammed his glass down on the counter and took her firmly by the elbow.

'Outside,' he hissed.

She went easily, grinning triumphantly around her as he propelled her towards the exit. He was vaguely aware that across the room the table of his work colleagues were rubbernecking in unison to watch, Alice included. He'd have to try and defuse the situation as best he could now and then get back in there and do some serious making up if he wanted to salvage the evening with Alice. If that meant announcing their relationship to the table, he'd have to do it.

He rounded on Ellie as soon as they were out in the lobby.

'What the hell was all that about? Why all the lies?' he asked her. His hair was all his own, he'd never used fake tan and no amount of money could have induced him to do something as girly as waxing.

Ellie looked at him defiantly.

'I was warning them off,' she said. 'Trouble is, you're so bloody perfect I had to make up some faults.'

He rubbed his forehead wearily with a thumb and forefinger.

'And you turned up here just to do that? You're stalking me now, is that it?'

'Don't flatter yourself,' she spat. 'I'm out with friends. I'm well over you. But when I saw you at the bar playing the same old game the opportunity was too good to pass up. Same old Harry. On to the next one-night stand.'

For the first time the hurt in her voice actually registered. To be fair, the last time he'd spoken to her he'd been so consumed by anger over his trashed belongings that he hadn't really considered how she might have been feeling. He took a closer look. Her face was twisted into an angry frown and he felt a sudden twinge of guilt. He had liked Ellie; she had been fun. The merry smile he remembered was a world away from the bitter way she looked now.

He had done that.

It occurred to him that he hadn't even apologised for the way things had turned out between them; he'd simply believed their relationship had been as casual to her as it was to him—in fact had blamed her for making too much out of it.

Was this what a conscience felt like?

'Ellie, I'm sorry,' he said, on impulse. 'For the way things turned out between us.'

She gave him a cynical look.

"Course you are, Harry. Am I ruining your evening—is that it? Need to get me out of the way so you can get on with finding the next girl?'

He held his hands up and shook his head.

'I'm not here to pull women. It's just a work thing.'

A cold pause. She made no response.

'I know I treated you badly and I'm sorry,' he said. 'I behaved like a total jerk. I didn't think for a second about your feelings.'

Her face took on an amazed expression and he felt slightly piqued. Was it *that* hard to believe that he was a decent guy?

'Seriously?' she said.

He nodded, smiling in what he hoped was a reassuring way and, too late, he saw the sudden spark of hope light up in her eyes. Before he could put any space between them she'd moved in and thrown her arms around him.

'I knew it,' she whispered into his shoulder. 'Deep down, I knew you'd see sense.'

He stared down in horror as she lifted her head and planted a kiss on his lips.

As the door from the bar opened behind him he finally wrenched himself free. Ellie switched her gaze over his shoulder.

'Harry?' Alice said. 'What's going on?'

He felt a lurch of nausea in his stomach because he knew how this would look to her. How she would *assume* it looked. Giving a damn about that wasn't a sensation he was used to.

It dawned on him suddenly that what was meant to be a great laugh of a bachelor lifestyle was really not much fun any more. Was this what he'd turned into—someone who trampled roughshod over people's feelings and never got to know anyone beyond the most superficial of levels? He wondered what the hell he'd ever thought was good about living that way.

'*Nothing* is going on!' he snapped, looking pointedly at Ellie as he put a good couple of paces between them.

The hopeful light in Ellie's eyes went instantly out. He caught a glimpse of her hurt expression as she put her head down and took a huge hitching breath, then she pushed past him back into the bar and was gone. It could have been worse. At least she didn't say anything to Alice. Then again, she'd said and done enough already.

The agonised expression on Alice's face tugged painfully at his heart. He could feel her regard sliding through his fingers like sand.

'Who was she?' Alice asked, her face pale and tight.

She's my ex-girlfriend who's been hell-bent on revenge since I dumped her like a bag of rubbish. Oh, yes, that would sound just great.

'She's nobody,' he said.

A frown. And the hurt expression was replaced by one of stony coldness.

'For nobody, you seemed to know her awfully well.'

'She temped at Innova for a while.'

She flung a hand up.

'I knew it! She's one of your exes. What, did you decide on an action replay?'

The unfairness of that comment riled him and he remembered with a hot stab of jealousy that she too had been ramping up her social interaction back in there.

'She came on to me, not the other way around,' he snapped. 'Which you might have noticed if you weren't so busy flirting yourself. You were totally surrounded in there.'

She stared at him, eyes wide and incredulous.

'Don't be ridiculous,' she snapped. 'I had no choice but to try and socialise since my *date* for the evening disappeared to flirt at the bar. And then, next up, he disappears outside with a pert blonde. I don't know why I'm even surprised— we both know you're just waiting for the next best thing to come along. And you certainly had your pick tonight.'

This was what she thought of him. And she had the weight of his past reputation to prove her point. He felt a surge of angry frustration.

She began to shrug herself into her jacket.

'What are you doing?'

'Isn't it obvious? I'm going home. I've had enough.' She glanced up at him. 'I don't need this. We're not even a proper couple. This is just a…a *warm-up*!'

That last dismissive comment really tore at him. He meant nothing to her beyond a few sample dates and now she was bailing? His heart plummeted with such sudden force it made him gasp for breath. She pushed open the door to the street and a rush of cold air filled the lobby. He darted after her as she crossed the pavement and raised an arm to hail a taxi.

'It wasn't what you think,' he shouted. Just this need to protest was alien to him. Why did he care so much what she thought of him? Why didn't he just let the bet slide, forget about the money, forget about the whole thing? Nothing was worth this much grief.

But he had a lot more than money staked on this now and convincing her that he'd changed seemed nigh on impossible.

A taxi pulled up beside her. She turned back to him, her face set.

'OK, fine. Is she or isn't she an ex of yours?'

He couldn't lie to her. Not to her. Not now.

'She is, but—'

'And did I not just see the pair of you kiss? Or was I hallucinating?'

He threw his hands up in exasperation.

'You did, but—'

'Then it *is* what I think,' she snapped. 'I've seen and heard enough.' She yanked the door of the taxi open and got in. 'Enjoy your evening.'

The door slammed and she was gone.

'Let me get this straight,' Tilly said, pushing her red hair back from her face. 'You saw him kissing another woman and you're actually *debating* whether you might have got it wrong. What have you done with the real Alice Ford?'

Alice stopped pacing the sitting room long enough to speak.

'She's one of his ex-girlfriends. He tried to insist it was all down to her, said she came on to him. And now I think about it he did seem to be trying to fight her off. I didn't hang around to hear him out and now...' she clenched her fists at the ceiling in frustration '...now I don't know what the hell to think. I don't even know why I'm giving him a second thought—his reputation should speak for itself, right?'

She looked at Tilly for reassurance.

'Not necessarily. Maybe he's changed.'

Not the answer she was looking for.

'Oh, honestly, people don't really change, do they? This is Harry Stephens we're talking about. Not all men are like lovely, straight-down-the-line Julian, you know.'

She could do without one of Tilly's rational chats right now. When her stomach was churning like this with hurt and confusion. What she needed was a pat on the back and to be told she'd done the right thing. An offer to break out a bottle of wine and a tub of ice cream might be nice too.

Tilly grinned.

'That's what you get when you go out with someone who believes in karma. And I did offer to set you up with one of Julian's friends, remember? Someone with no hidden agenda, with scruples and a moral code. You declined. Which tells me that perhaps straight-down-the-line doesn't float your boat as much as you'd like it to.'

Alice ran a distracted hand through her hair. Maybe that was the problem. Despite her past she was still drawn to exactly the same kind of man as she always was: smart, funny, exciting and challenging. And because of her past, the payoff for that had to be lack of trust.

It was true she'd done her own share of flirting too, swept along by the idea of playing him at his own game. Despite her protestations to Harry it had actually been fun to be the centre of attention for a change. Maybe she just hadn't liked it when he'd tipped the balance of power a bit too far his way. Maybe he was telling the truth. Perhaps he had changed, as Tilly said. Maybe for the right woman he could be a keeper after all. Was she just jumping to conclusions and thinking the worst of him because of her own damn baggage?

But his past spoke for itself, didn't it?

She'd reacted to the thought that she was being played by him by doing exactly what she'd done when Simon had betrayed her. She'd got herself out of the situation as quickly as possible. She hadn't left time for lame excuses. Why prolong it? Why drag out the humiliation?

She so desperately wanted to believe she'd moved on from that awful time, that she was stronger now. And maybe the only way to prove that would be by giving him the chance to explain. She wasn't operating blindly here, was she? She was still in full mental control. She could hear him out and make a proper decision, like the calm controlled woman she was now.

She grabbed her jacket from the back of her chair on her way back out.

CHAPTER NINE

*Rule #9 A player will involve you in his home life as
little as possible. Don't be surprised if he finds excuses
not to invite you back to his place.*

RIGHT UP UNTIL Alice got out of the taxi at the end of Harry's
road, she intended to knock on the door like a grown-up and
give him the chance to discuss the evening rationally. Unfortunately, somewhere during the short walk, sensibility
was crushed underfoot by paranoia. Since she'd left him at
the bar there had been a wall of silence. No follow-up calls
to protest his innocence. No chasing after her in a taxi. And
suddenly she couldn't shake the feeling that he might have
given up on talking her round because he'd taken the lean
blonde woman home with him.

How could she trust her own judgement? When had she
been such an expert on character-guessing? When she'd
dreamed of marriage to a man who turned out to be ex-
ploiting her for fun? Add in Harry's reputation and it would
never be enough for her to just give him the benefit of the
doubt. That was Simon's legacy. Listening to whatever explanation he wanted to give just wouldn't cut the mustard.
If she was to be sure, she had no choice but to check up on
him. That was the price of peace.

And so instead of walking up the path to his front door

like any normal human being and pressing the doorbell, she was now teetering on the top of a wobbling pile of crates in his back garden, craning to see through a chink in his curtains.

The worst thing of all was that she could no longer deny it. Pressing the doorbell would have meant she was still in control of her emotions. Teetering like a lunatic in his back garden meant she was in too deep. She cared far too much now what his game was. Because if this visit was really only about her list of player behaviour, a knock on the front door would have done. The fact her insecurities had taken over meant the worst was true. She was falling for him.

She leaned forward and gripped the windowsill to give herself a few inches more leaning ability. Falling for him she might be, but she could still save herself. It wasn't too late to curb that now if her worst fears happened to be realised. The lights were on. He was obviously home. The question now was whether he was home alone or whether he'd brought the blonde along for company. Or maybe even picked up someone else entirely. It had been more than two hours since she'd left him in the bar, plenty of time for a player like him to pick up an entire harem.

It rankled that he had never invited her back to his place. She thought of Arabella, who'd left her earrings here. Obviously he hadn't been above taking her home with him. Maybe he reserved his shag-pad for one-night stands only—that way he could pursue two women at a time, right? The easy ones could come straight back here, and the ones who didn't immediately fall at his feet could be wined and dined. She could see plates, mugs, some pots and pans through the gap in the curtains. A pigsty admittedly, but undeniably a kitchen.

She could hear faint sounds inside, too indistinguishable to work out if he was in there with someone or if the TV was on. Another surge of paranoia made her shift her weight.

And suddenly there he was, in the room, gorgeous as ever in jeans and dark blue shirt. She watched as he opened a cupboard and took out a glass. She framed her eyes against the window with her hands to try and get a better view, see if he took down a second glass, then maybe a bottle of champagne would appear and then…

Without warning, although the wobbly danger signs had been there all along, there was a shift beneath her knees and the crates below her crashed in a crumbling mess of sharp corners and hip-scraping sides into a haphazard pile. She went down with them, unable to stop an anguished squawk as she lost her footing, and ended up lying on her back staring up at the starry sky. There were bruises all over her and, worse, the burn of embarrassment rushed through her like fire as the back door opened with a bang and suddenly he was there, looking down at her with an incredulous expression on his face.

'You only had to knock.'

Unfortunately there was no ladylike way of clawing your way out of a pile of crates. Alice ended up heaving her way out onto the damp grass like a hippo. She looked up at him, towering above her in the slanting glow of light from the open back door, his hair lightly tousled, an amused expression on the chiselled face, and wondered if there was a nearby stone big enough for her to crawl under. It didn't matter now if he turned out to be a keeper in player's clothing, because she'd blown it.

'I can explain,' she said, reaching out to take his proffered hand. He pulled her to her feet in one easy tug and then she was next to him, his gaze holding hers, the clouds of their breath mingling. Her heart raced.

'I look forward to that,' he said, his voice dangerously neutral, giving no reaction away. 'Just let me grab a jacket.

I'll take you for a drink, there's a good pub at the end of the road, and you can go for your life. I'm sure it will be a gripping story.'

He turned back towards the door, and as she digested what he'd said and realised what he was doing humiliation was pushed out in its entirety by one thought of absolute clarity.

He doesn't want me inside his house.

She stumbled after him, grimacing at the ache in her bones from her ungainly fall, and grabbed his arm.

'No need to go to the pub,' she said. 'I'm here now. A cup of coffee will do. Let's just get inside out of the cold.'

Although frankly she wasn't feeling the bite of the autumn evening one bit. Her whole body seemed to be boiling up with anger. Who did he have in there that he didn't want her to see? Had he left the blonde in his bed?

'Pub's much nicer,' he said, his face inscrutable. 'I forgot to get any milk in and the place is a tip.'

'Black coffee is fine and I don't give a toss about a bit of mess,' she said, not letting go of his arm. She thought that might be enough, but still he didn't invite her in and stood blocking the way.

Enough was enough.

She dropped his arm, sidestepped him neatly and walked across damp grass onto the gravel path, heading towards the door.

'Alice,' he called after her. 'Alice, please don't go in there.'

'Who is she?' she snapped over her shoulder at him, almost at the door now. 'Your ex from tonight, the Innova temp? Or just someone you picked up after I…oh, my flippin life!'

The smell hit her as she made it through the door. Inside was a galley kitchen with a table at one end, a sink full of washing-up, yet she didn't register any of it because it felt as if only one of her five senses was working. The gagging stench of rotting dead fish assaulted her and extinguished all coherent thought. It was so dense the air felt almost soupy with it. She clapped a revolted hand over her mouth and turned back to him as he caught up with her. She vaguely registered that his face was apologetic.

'What in the name of hell is that *smell*?' She gasped, shoving him blindly aside so she could stick her head out of the back door and take a few gulps of fresh air.

'I wish to hell I knew,' he said.

She moved outside to stand on the doorstep. She could still pick up the stench from here but it was diluted enough by the fresh air outside that she could at least think coherently.

'Why don't we just go to the pub?' he said again.

She remembered why she was here. Surely the smell didn't permeate the whole house.

'Is there someone else in here? Is that why you're so reluctant to invite me in?'

'That's why you were lurking in my garden in the dark instead of ringing the doorbell? You think I've got some other woman holed up in here somewhere?'

Embarrassment at the fact he'd caught her gurning through his window made a comeback.

'Alice,' he said slowly, as if talking to a toddler. 'There is no one in here apart from me. If I haven't invited you over it's because I didn't think you'd particularly enjoy spending time in my house when it smells like something's died in here.'

'Oh,' she said in a small voice.

'What do you think—that I've got some woman hidden in my wardrobe? Go on and look,' he said, moving aside so she had easy access past him. 'Go on, check it out. You'll find a bit of a mess but you won't find any other woman.' His blue eyes were fixed on hers. 'I'm not interested in any other woman.'

Her stomach gave a slow and melting flip. Part of her, the

part that kept glancing back instead of looking forwards, wanted to push past him and ransack the place. Yet she knew if she succumbed to that desire it would be a regression. And for Pete's sake, it wasn't as if his excuse weren't plausible. She had the godawful stench filling her nostrils to prove it.

She took a deep breath and forced herself to think rationally.

'I don't need to go through your cupboards,' she said. 'I'll take your word for it.'

He sighed in a finally-she-sees-sense way.

'OK, then,' he said. 'Bring on the explanation. In fact, you don't need to. It's pretty obvious why you were lurking in my garden. You were suspicious because of what happened tonight and you decided to check it out—is that it?'

She pulled her coat more tightly around her and folded her arms against the cold. She avoided his eyes. No point denying it.

'That's pretty much it,' she said.

He nodded.

'You could have just asked me straight out,' he said.

She wondered for a crazy moment if she would ever be the kind of person for whom asking straight out would be good enough. Or if she was doomed to mistrust everyone and everything until the end of time.

'The problem with that is your track record,' she said, on the defensive because she'd made such a fool of herself. 'Based on your past and the way you and that blonde disappeared for some *private time…*' she made sarcastic speech marks in the air with her fingers '…do you really blame me for thinking if I asked you outright you might not have given me a straight answer?'

Silence while he looked down at his feet and ran both hands through his hair. Then he sighed and looked up at her.

'Ellie is an ex-girlfriend,' he said. 'I told you that. There's absolutely nothing between us now.'

She pulled a face.

'You were in a clinch. I know what I saw.'

'You saw *Ellie* kiss *me*. But you didn't see what went on before that and you were too determined to think the worst of me to give me five minutes to explain.'

A warm flush crept into her cheeks because he had a point and she knew it.

'This is just a few dates to you, right?' he carried on. 'If that's really all it is, if you don't really care one way or the other, then why go through all this cloak-and-dagger stuff? If you don't feel you can trust me, don't come here trying to catch me out, just bail.'

A sharp prickling at the very back of her throat made her swallow hard. Because it no longer was just a few dates to her and, although admitting it to herself felt like pulling fingernails, she didn't want to bail.

'Trust is…' she took a deep breath '…well, it's a big ask, that's all.'

He took her hand in his then, and the prickly throat almost made a comeback.

'There *is* no other woman,' he said. 'There won't be. Not while I'm seeing you. I don't cheat. If I'm not happy I end it before I move on.' He looked over her shoulder, through the door into the foul-smelling kitchen.

'Trouble is, with Ellie I left ending it a bit too long.'

He grabbed a couple of the crates and turned them upside down, then sat down and tugged her down next to him. It was a perfect clear autumn night and moonlight washed the small garden in silver. Behind him golden light from his kitchen pooled outside the back door. Her senses were so focused on him that she barely registered the chill air.

He looked her in the eye.

'You want to know what's going on between Ellie and me?'

Her heart began to pick up the pace as she nodded her head.

'I haven't told anyone about this.'

Hideous scenarios paraded through her head, making it spin. Was she pregnant? Were they secretly married? Her heart felt suddenly like lead. She bit her bottom lip and waited for the bombshell.

'I'm the victim of a woman scorned,' he said.

For a moment she couldn't quite comprehend what he'd just said.

'You're what?'

'Ellie is a vengeful ex-girlfriend. A bunny-boiler.' He paused. 'And she really got me good. No one knows about it. Except for you now.'

She stared at him. His blue eyes were totally clear and because the look in them was one of weary resignation she bit back the compulsion to laugh. How ironic that Mr Love-Them-And-Leave-Them was fed up with being messed about by an ex.

'Of all the things I expected you to say, *that* didn't even make the list,' she said.

As a past member of the woman-scorned club herself, curiosity was eating her up as to what this Ellie had actually done.

'What happened?' she prompted.

He shrugged.

'I dated her for a few months. We went out, had a good time—at least I thought we had a good time—and then—'

'What?'

'She started to talk about next steps, moving in together, meeting her parents, that kind of thing.'

This time she couldn't suppress a laugh.

'Let me guess—you ran for the hills.'

His lips twitched into a small smile at that.

'I didn't exactly run for the hills but I told her I didn't want anything serious, I thought it had run its course between us…'

'You'd like to be just friends, blah blah, the usual.'

'Exactly.'

'How did she take it?'

'Like a total lunatic,' he said. 'She came round to my place to pick up a few of her things that she'd left there. I was in the kitchen, keeping out of the way. I didn't realise until after she'd gone that she'd shredded my entire wardrobe and tipped coffee dregs over my laptop.'

'Oh, wow.'

'I know,' he said. 'It gets worse. A couple of days later and my car was keyed. Really badly. It cost me a fortune to get a respray.'

'That was her too?'

'I don't know for certain,' he said. 'But, yeah, I think so.'

She sighed and ran a hand through her hair. Try as she might to feel sympathy for him, there was no getting away from the fact she could relate to this girl, this Ellie. Another girl just like her, who'd had the confidence and self-respect crushed out of her by some man just because he was out to have fun. There was a brief dark moment as she remembered the place she'd been in when she'd found out that the pictures intended for Simon's eyes only had been shared out like sweets. No wonder that she could empathise with this Ellie after that. If he was expecting commiserations he'd come to the wrong girl.

'Thing is, Harry, you kind of had it coming,' she said. 'There are at least half a dozen women in the office who'd probably give that girl a medal.'

She waited for his angry reaction.

'I know,' he said.

'You do?' Not what she'd expected and she couldn't hide her surprise.

'Yes. My first thought was to call the police, press charges, especially on the car damage. You have no idea how pissed I was about that. But then I thought about it and I realised I had to take some responsibility. I just hadn't seen that she was setting so much store by our relationship. I should have been clearer with her from the start. To me it was only ever going to be a laugh and I messed up, let it run on too long, let her think it was more than it was. She was obviously reading a whole lot more into it than that.'

'And tonight?' she said, catching her breath.

He paused.

'Tonight I realised how upset she must have been to do those things. It wasn't my finest hour. I feel awful, like I've messed with her head. I tried to apologise, tell her that I never meant to hurt her—'

'And?'

'She thought I'd had some change of heart, that I'd suddenly seen the light and wanted to get back together. She kissed me before I knew what the hell was happening and then you showed up. I can see how it must have looked.'

For a moment she couldn't say anything. It all sounded so plausible. Then he reached for her hand and the look of regret in his eyes made her heart melt.

She looked down at her hand, encircled in his, and in that moment she accepted the risk, took his explanation at face value.

She stood up and walked towards the house.

'You're going inside? Without a gas mask?' he called after her.

'I've had an idea,' she said.

* * *

'How long has it been here?' she asked him, grimacing and sniffing the air as she made her way through to his sitting room. Pleasant bay-fronted room, the floors stripped back to boards, a large leather sofa and flat-screen TV. Very single-guy.

'First noticed it about a week ago,' he said. 'Just a whiff of it at first, not enough to make me think there was any kind of problem. But when I got back from Manchester this afternoon it was a million times worse. It's especially bad downstairs in the sitting room and kitchen.'

'Your kitchen isn't exactly an example of perfect hygiene,' she said.

'I haven't got round to washing up,' he protested. 'My fridge and cupboards are perfectly clean—you can check.'

She did, walking back to the kitchen and opening cupboard doors. So he was right. And the smell definitely seemed worse in the sitting room, and undoubtedly it was fishy.

'And when did Ellie last come over here? Your woman scorned.'

'She hasn't been over here since she turned my wardrobe into rags.'

He followed her as she walked back down the hall and paced the sitting room, sniffing the air.

'And it ended a few weeks ago, did you say?'

He nodded as she dragged a chair across to the window sill and climbed on it.

'What the hell are you doing?'

'Solving your problem,' she said. 'Finding the source.'

He watched her with a bemused expression as she reached up to the curtain pole and unscrewed the pelmet with one hand, the other covering her mouth and nose.

'Aaargh!'

The smell instantly intensified to the point of unbearable, so strong it made her eyes water. Half laughing and half grimacing, he was suddenly across the room, sliding an arm around her waist and lifting her down to the floor. Her heart skipped a beat at his sudden closeness as he grabbed her hand and pulled her out to the hallway, opening the front door to let the crisp clean night air in. She leaned against the doorway laughing with him.

'There's your answer,' she gasped, gesturing back inside. 'Prawns in the curtain pole. Now all you need to do is clean the thing out or get rid of it and the smell will be gone.'

He looked down at her, incredulous expression on his face.

'How the hell did you know?'

She looked down at her fingernails.

'It came to me just now. When you were telling me about Ellie and the things she did. It just suddenly occurred to me that the smell might be a revenge thing too. At some point in the last couple of weeks—I'm guessing when she came to collect her stuff and shredded your wardrobe—she unscrewed that curtain pole and filled it with fresh prawns. Nothing happened for a couple of weeks until the prawns started to go off, then within days you've got the stench from hell. A few more days and you'd probably have had pest control out, had the floorboards up. But you still wouldn't have found it.'

She glanced back up to see him looking at her curiously.

'It hadn't crossed my mind that it could be down to her.'

'You haven't heard from her for a few weeks so you assumed it was over with. That's what you wanted to think. You wanted to dismiss her behaviour as just a brief overreaction to your break-up, whereas I can see where she's coming from. Sort of,' she added quickly, so he wouldn't think she was some kind of stalker from hell too.

He was shaking his head in disbelief.

'No problem,' she said. 'You've found it now. You just need to clean the pole out and problem solved.'

She made a move to go back into the house, thinking she might open some windows, but he reached out and touched her wrist, gently held it.

'You can *sort of see where she's coming from*?' he said.

She turned back slowly, looking down at his hand on her arm, and saw with a flash what this actually said about her, what he was probably thinking. Not an hour ago she'd been secretly peering in at his back window and now she wasn't exactly sympathetic about his relationship revenge.

She looked up at him in the cool darkness, the crisp air making her breath cloud. She could see his blue eyes in the golden light spilling out from the hallway and she could see concern there, not confrontation. Yet she still couldn't face the humiliation of telling him the reason why she could empathise with this Ellie. She kept it vague.

'Let's just say I had a bad relationship. And maybe I can understand why Ellie might have wanted to get her own back. And yes, there's a part of me that thinks good on her, good on her for standing up for herself. There were times when I wished I had the balls to rip up Simon's wardrobe or send him pizzas that he hadn't ordered...'

He was looking at her with his eyebrows raised and she realised she was doing herself no favours here if she wanted to dig herself out of the stalker mould.

'But the point is, I never *did* anything like that. I never would. Not because I didn't want to be mean or hurt him, or even because he might call the police and have me warned off.' She felt a little click in her throat because she was getting upset. 'I didn't do any of it because I knew it wouldn't make me feel better. It wouldn't change what he'd done.' She sighed. 'But I'm not going to lie—I can see Ellie might have got a certain satisfaction from doing these things.'

A long pause.

She waited. Waited for him to wrap the evening up. Call her a taxi. One way or another, he'd be running a mile now.

'Wait here a sec,' he said.

He disappeared inside the house and she jumped as she heard windows bang shut, saw the lights go off inside. He returned within five minutes with his keys, jacket and wallet.

'Come on,' he said, unlocking the car.

'I'll get the Tube,' she called after him, sudden pride kicking in. Why the hell should she care what his judgement of her was? As if he were some kind of icon for relationship etiquette! 'I don't need a lift.'

He stood next to the car, driver's door open, the light from the car backlighting his face.

'I'm not taking you home.' A pause. 'At least not yet.' A shrug. 'Unless you want to go home, in which case you're insane if you think I'd let you take the Underground at this time of night on your own.'

His concern made her stomach feel soft. Even if it was going to be short-lived.

She walked down the path, joined him by the car.

'Where are we going then?'

'Somewhere we can talk that doesn't smell like a fish market,' he said. 'I can't stand that smell a second longer. I'll book myself in somewhere tonight and sort the house out tomorrow. We can have a drink and then I'll drop you home.'

Rule #10 Sleep with him at your peril. The moment he gets what he wants you become dispensable.

Not for Harry a Travelodge or bargain B&B joint. Half an hour later and he'd booked a room in a luxurious boutique hotel near Regent's Park. She found herself sitting on a squashy velvet sofa next to the ornate fireplace, her stomach in knots because across the room there was a bed. She held her glass of wine in her hands to stop herself fidgeting. The subtle lighting in the room made him look more gorgeous than ever, light stubble defining his jaw, tiny smile lines etched at the corner of his eyes.

'I know what you're thinking,' she said. 'But I'm not some mad stalker. Peering through your back window was more about me than it was about you. I wanted to believe you at the bar when you told me there was nothing going on between you and Ellie, but trusting my own judgement is so hard. I've screwed up so badly in the past. I wasn't stalking, I was…double-checking.'

He sat down opposite her, his own glass in his hand, and she saw with relief that he was smiling.

'Is that because of your ex or because of me?' he said.

He waited but she didn't answer. His expression was gentle.

'I don't think for a moment that you're some crazy stalker. I think you're someone who—for whatever reason—finds it hard to trust, to let anyone in. What exactly did he do to make you that insecure?'

She looked at her wine in the glass, soft gold in the flickering light of the votives on the table, and tried to remember the last time she'd actually verbalised what had happened with Simon. She found she couldn't. Tilly knew of course, she knew everything about Alice. But with the job at Innova she'd simply reinvented herself and built up a whole new bank of friends and colleagues. None of them knew about her past. Those that did had been left behind in Dorset along with her mother and her insane cycle of unsuitable relationships. She'd figured that London would be far enough. Did she really want to unearth all that pain again by entrusting what had happened to someone who inhabited that new life?

Yet Harry had proved her wrong. There was no other woman. She'd let her paranoia get in the way.

And maybe that was driving the problem. Maybe by not talking, not thinking about what Simon had done she'd buried her resentment deep inside her, where it festered like the prawns in Harry's curtain pole. But letting it out all this time later, just like the stench that had permeated Harry's house, would be so much worse.

His opinion of her right now couldn't be clearer. After his encounter with prawn-girl Ellie he wasn't likely to be interested in an insecure woman who needed endless reassurance. Needy and clingy with revenge potential. She couldn't bear to be thought of as that. Worse, she couldn't bear *him* to think of her like that. All that was left was for him to bail and she wasn't about to tell him her darkest secret when he had to be on the brink of showing her the door.

At least she could get in first with that and salvage what self-respect she had left.

'Maybe I should go,' she said, putting her glass down on the low table next to her. She took a deep breath. 'I'm sorry for behaving like an idiot,' she said. 'I look at the way I've behaved with you, pouring coffee over your head, peering through your window, and you must think I'm some kind of lunatic.' She gave a helpless laugh. 'Even *I* think I'm being crazy but it all seems so damn *rational* at the time.'

He smiled at her and she forced herself to carry on.

'You were right when you said we should disregard everything in the past and just think about us. Default should be trust, until it's proven otherwise.' She sighed. 'But I can't do that. My default setting is broken. And there's nothing I can do about it.'

She began to stand up, but before she could get to her feet he was in front of her. He knelt on the floor, his gaze at eye level, blue eyes locked on to hers. His hand found hers, his fingers entwining softly with her own. She looked into his eyes and saw no distaste, no anger. Nothing but concern for her. And something else that made her catch her breath.

Desire.

'It doesn't have to be like that,' he said.

As he reached up and stroked her cheek softly she didn't pull away. Her heart was pounding in her chest and her stomach was a soft squiggly mass of anticipation. Three years since she'd been in such an intimate situation and all thought of control melted away as her own desire took over, melding her firmly in the present. No reference to what had gone before and no room for thoughts about what she stood to lose if she'd made the wrong judgement here.

There was no crushing against her, no forcing things forward at some superhuman pace. His touch was languorous and slow. Always hesitant, letting her know by his tentative movements that stop could be invoked at any moment, waiting for her approval at every turn.

If she'd allowed herself to imagine this moment it would have featured him as the driving force, pushing ever onward to his conclusion. Now she found the opposite.

For a long instant he looked into her eyes, daring her to stop things. Then slowly, deliciously, his mouth was against hers, his fingers softly stroking their way into her hair, tilting her face to meet his. His other hand slid gently around her waist. The deep spicy scent of his aftershave filled her senses. He moved from his knees to sit on the floor and she felt the gentlest of tugging as he pulled her into his lap, the chiffon skirt of her dress crinkling upwards and pooling softly around them.

She'd expected him to take full control. At speed. Had actually steeled herself against it. And now the passion, the delicious slowness of it all, brought a rush of desire that was new to her. Had she ever felt this level of longing for anyone before? Had her body ever been sensation central like this before? Every nerve ending in her body felt zingily alive.

The novelty that she was in charge here, that she could say how fast or how slow, when to stop, filled her with delight. Slowly at first but gaining in confidence, she kissed him back, letting her hands slide underneath his shirt across warm skin and taut muscle. She circled her hips lightly against him, feeling his arousal and indulging it until at last he took gentle control, standing up and lifting her into his arms, his hands sliding around her as she locked her legs behind him. He carried her across the room to the bed.

Afterwards Alice lay nestled perfectly in the crook of his arm as if that spot were designed to be a perfect fit just for her. The only light in the room flickered from the candles grouped in the hearth and on the table. She rested her head against his chest, listening to the heartbeat beneath, and squeezed her eyes tightly shut. She'd been swept up in the deliciousness of it, the infinite tenderness of him. When he'd held her gently and looked into her eyes, holding her gaze while they moved as one, there had been no room in her mind for cynical thoughts about his motivation—those thoughts had been floating somewhere in the stratosphere, banished by the depth of pleasure he invoked in her.

Her own heartbeat now wouldn't quit. And not because she was still riding high on the last hour, but because now the deliciousness was over it was time to deal with the fallout.

Likely next move: Harry begins to distance himself. Awful.

Alternative next move: If he happened to have a spot on the bet pool she'd just handed him victory on a plate. Worse.

She squeezed her eyes tightly shut and scrabbled around

desperately for a likely next move from him that wouldn't put her life all the way back to square one.

There was none.

What the hell had she gone and done?

CHAPTER TEN

S<small>HE SHOULD GET</small> out of here. Right now.

Her clothes were all over the room.

There was no way in this universe that Alice could face climbing boldly out of this bed and walking stark naked to pick up her things while he watched her every move. No matter that in the last hour or so he'd kissed her in places she'd never been kissed before, he hadn't actually *seen* her naked, had he? Even in the dim light, without the confidence of the moment shyness took control.

She waited, wide awake and trying not to tense up, for him to fall asleep. She breathed in the warm musky scent of his skin and felt the smooth muscle of his body against hers. She listened, trying not to tense, for his breathing to even out and then added an extra ten minutes for good measure. Then she eased herself bit by bit first from his embrace and then from the bed, and then she speed-tiptoed around the shadowy room dodging furniture and picking up her clothes.

Her panties had somehow ended up hanging on a corner of the trouser press and she snatched them back and stepped quickly into them, the words *proof required* flashing like a neon sign in her mind. If he really was a part of the bet, she intended to do everything in her power not to leave a trace that she was ever here. If asked she would simply deny this ever happened, deny that she had come here, and let's not forget she had the weight of her ice-queen reputation to back her up. Who would believe on just his say-so that Ice-Queen Ford would ever go to bed with the biggest player in the office?

Providing *proof required* was not going to be that easy for him.

She put the rest of her clothes on quickly in the bathroom, then, finally satisfied that she'd left nothing to chance, she crossed the bedroom to pick up her bag and coat from the sofa. Turning to head for the door, she was just congratulating herself on doing all she could to dig herself out of the situation when he unexpectedly turned on the overhead light.

She froze in the sudden brightness and for a moment considered bolting out of the door anyway. She pulled herself together. Dignity meant not running away like some stupid teenager. She turned to face him.

He was standing by the bed wearing nothing but shorts, leaning against the wall next to the light switch. She tried hard to keep her eyes on his face and not let them dip below chest level. It was nigh on impossible. Abs like that really shouldn't be allowed. And to look at his heavily muscled arms was to remember what they felt like encircling her. She swallowed hard to get some moisture back in her mouth. His hair was tousled into spikes and a small smile lifted the corner of his mouth, creasing his blue eyes lightly. Her stomach felt traitorously melty. It had all been so much easier to label him villain in the semi-darkness. She saw him watching her with a shrewd attention that contained no hint of sleepiness, making it clear he'd probably been awake the whole time.

'I thought you were asleep,' she said.

'You're leaving?'

She shrugged. 'I have to get back. I have an early meeting tomorrow.'

Harry noticed she was avoiding his eyes and edging towards the door.

So that was it. She was pre-empting his next move, assuming that taking her to bed would be swiftly followed by him losing interest. Not this time.

'You're bailing?' he said.

'I'm beating you to it.'

'You've spent the last three years bailing. I thought that's what all this was about, putting all that behind you, getting back out there.'

'All this?'

'Us.'

Just saying the word brought it home how different this was with her. How different she was. When had he last used that term? When it was him and Susie against the world. Since she'd grown up and started her own life it had been him. Just him. Until now.

'What "us" are you talking about?' she said. 'The "us" that have been out a few times, had a laugh, slept together? Because I don't see how any of that distinguishes me from any of the stream of girls you've been with. The only difference is I'm not waiting around for you to get bored and jump ship. I'm getting in first.'

Her hair was tousled from the bed and her eye make-up was smudgier, making her brown eyes look huge. She held his gaze boldly, all bravado. He crushed a surge of desire for her, knowing that to make this about sex would be to confirm all her stereotypical beliefs about him. She obviously thought that was all he was interested in.

A couple of weeks ago this situation would have been gold. When he'd talked her into dating him in the Ladies at work, this would have been the end result of his dreams. Fun couple of weeks, great sex, and now he didn't even have to do the dumping. She was walking away, leaving the path open for him to just waltz into the office in the morning and collect a nice fat stash of cash and pats on the back from his mates.

So how come the perfect result now made it feel as if his heart was about to be put through a shredder?

He'd fallen for her.

The problem was going to be convincing her of that.

He crossed the room towards her and took her hand in his, entwined his fingers with hers and tugged her close against him. He could smell the faint scent of her hair and the last couple of hours rushed deliciously back through his mind, firing him right back up. She stuffed her bag and coat in between them, effectively keeping him at arm's length.

'Don't go,' he said. 'Stay over. I'll drop you home early in the morning so you can change for work.'

This must be part of his policy, then. Well, Alice supposed, if you were going to have a short-term fling or a one-night stand, it made sense to squash as much back-to-back sex into that space of time as you could. Though, her mind faltered, if he was in on the bet surely once would be enough. She rubbed her forehead with the heel of her hand. She was so confused. She'd made a huge mistake by sleeping with him. She was in far too deep. This went way beyond a dating experiment.

Best thing she could possibly do now was put a stop to it and make a swift exit. *Short-term plan:* get out of the hotel room and put plenty of space between her and Harry Stephens. Examining her heart for wounds would have to come later.

'This never happened,' she said.

The look on his face was one of pure surprise.

'What?'

'This,' she said, sweeping her hands in an all-encompassing gesture. 'You. Me. Here tonight. It didn't happen. Erase it from your mind. Pretend I just went home after we were at your house. I'll do the same. Let's just get back to the way things were before. Friends.' She considered for a moment. 'Actually, scratch that. Workmates.'

She made a move for the door and made an unsuccessful attempt to operate the twisting lock.

'Wait!' His voice was genuinely bemused. 'What are you talking about, this never happened?' He put a hand out and gently touched her shoulder, turning her back to face him. 'Will you stop fiddling with the door and talk to me?'

Harry could see from the anguished expression in her brown eyes that her impulse was to bolt, yet the way her breathing had sped up and the delicious way she bit her lower lip told him otherwise. He lifted a hand to stroke her hair back from her face, heat rising inside him again just at the feel of her skin beneath his fingers. Desire for her was tempered by a sense of hideous shame and hatred for himself. That she'd entrusted herself to him. That he'd wagered money on her. It burned in his chest, eating him up from the inside out.

It was meant to be a laugh. It was most definitely not meant to be like this.

'I know you're thinking that now we've had sex it's the beginning of the end,' he said.

Her face was inscrutable and she didn't answer.

'That's not what I want,' he said.

She put her head on one side and surveyed him.

'What is it that you want, then, Harry?' she said. 'A second round? An all-nighter maybe—may as well make the most of it as you've booked the hotel room, right?'

'This is different,' he said.

'This?'

The look in her eyes was cynical. He hated it.

'You and me,' he said.

She only looked at him, the scepticism still right there, and he took her hand and tugged her over to the sofa. He sat down and after a moment she followed suit, perching on the edge of the seat with her bag and coat still in her lap, ready to go.

He looked into her face, holding her gaze as he held her hand in his.

'All I ever wanted was to have a laugh,' he said. 'This decade was meant to be the polar opposite of the last one. I spent the latter half of my teens and the early part of my twenties looking forward to the day where I could make snap decisions, stay out all night, get on a plane at a moment's notice. All without thinking about responsibility to anyone else. I just wanted to have some fun.' She was watching him intently. 'And up until now that's just what this has been.'

'This?'

He made a sweeping gesture with his hand.

'My life. The way I've lived since I moved up to London.'

'And now?'

He held her gaze with his own, trying to communicate that he was serious, that this wasn't some put-on.

'When I started seeing you the rules were different. It was clear from the outset that you weren't about to get serious. A player, you called me—remember? The polar opposite of what you were looking for. And because I knew you were never going to want anything long term there was no need to keep a guard up or distance myself. I've got to know you. I don't usually let that happen. I've got to like your mad be-haviour—you're so strung out at work and underneath there's this smart, funny girl making me laugh and buoying me up.'

He had no idea if he was making any progress here at all. Her face gave nothing away. She was still listening though; she hadn't chosen the door. Not yet.

'I realised I haven't really got to know anyone since I've been here. That's been the payoff for keeping things fun—I never get to know anyone beyond the most basic stuff. And after a while that means one person becomes very much like the next.' He looked at her and shrugged. 'What the hell is fun about that?'

She didn't say anything, just looked at him wide-eyed.

'And now this thing with Ellie—I'd been kidding myself that if we were both adults, going into it with our eyes open, then I couldn't be blamed for her meltdown when it ended. I could kid myself like that because she never meant anything to me beyond short-term fun. Same with the other girls. None of them meant anything to me. But then tonight in that bar I watched you talking to John. I saw the way he was looking at you and paying you attention.' He looked into her eyes. 'I didn't like it.'

'It was down to you,' she protested. 'I was on a date with *you*. Don't you think I'd rather have been sitting and talking to you? You were totally surrounded and you didn't look like you minded one bit.'

How could he tell her he had wanted to keep their relationship low-key because he was afraid someone would have given away the bet? He groped for an alternative explanation.

'You wanted to start socialising again—that was the whole reason you went out with me. I thought you might want to mingle.'

Oh, yes, that sounded just great.

'It was a couple of drinks in a bar, not the Ambassador's Reception,' she snapped.

'It wouldn't have mattered where we were, don't you understand? Watching you tonight was the first time I understood why Ellie reacted the way she did.' He shook his head, still surprised himself by the revelation.

'I was jealous.'

He was jealous? Her heart wanted to soar with happiness at what that meant. Surely he would have just let her leave if she meant nothing more to him than a quickie. He certainly wouldn't have gone to the trouble of explaining himself to her. And there was that tiny niggling voice telling her that if he was still interested in her after tonight then he was very unlikely to be in it for a bet. Why keep seeing her once he'd bedded her if all it had been about was some stupid financial incentive? The temptation to just accept what he'd told her and let him take her back to bed was huge, but she reined in her skipping heart.

The caution of the past held her back. She needed time to think clearly, get some space. She'd done enough following of impulse for one night. If he was still as full-on as this to-morrow, maybe *then* she would believe him.

Standing up, she leaned down to give him a soft kiss. She squished the sparks it generated in her belly and moved a firm step backwards the moment she felt his hands begin to slide around her.

'I really have to go,' she said, trying to keep her breath even when she really wanted to pant. 'I'll see you tomorrow.'

Before all sense disappeared she left the room.

CHAPTER ELEVEN

Rule #11 What time slot is he working in? If he never plans to see you more than a week ahead, he's keeping his options open in case something better comes along.

TOMORROW HAD BEEN and gone. The weekend had been and gone. And with the passing of each hour in Harry's company trust grew a little more. At work they maintained a professional distance but it was only a matter of time before their relationship became common knowledge. She felt no need now to rush it; she had nothing to prove.

Cuddled up to him on her own sofa in her own little sitting room, Kevin the cat ousted, Alice felt happiness within her grasp. Things were full-on between them now.

'I've been thinking,' he said, nuzzling her neck.

She unpeeled his fingers from the remote control and turned the channel from the football to a soap opera. He stopped mid-nuzzle and leaned up on one elbow to glance at the TV and then at her, eyebrows raised. She waited for him to complain and when he smiled instead and went right back to cuddling up, her stomach gave another one of those melty flips. If anything said love it was letting her choose the channel during a World Cup qualifier.

'What about?'

'How about we take a break? Go away somewhere, just the two of us before Christmas starts to kick in.'

He curled his arms more tightly around her and she snuggled into him.

'A holiday?'

When had she last been away on holiday? She'd been away to a festival last year with Tilly. Two nights in a tent in the middle of a muddy field, queuing up for communal toilets and drinking mead. A hideous experience she had no intention of repeating. A luxury break with Harry was definitely more her thing. Plus the thought that Harry wanted to plan ahead and was obviously seeing them together long term filled her with joy. She beamed up into his face.

'Where shall we go?'

'Where would you like to go?'

'Barbados,' she said, aiming high.

He pulled a face.

'Too film-star.'

She rolled her eyes. How could anything be too film-star?

'OK, how about a bit closer to home. We could have a cosy weekend up in the Lakes.'

'*Too* close to home,' he said. 'Come on. Think of somewhere you've always dreamed of going.'

'Venice,' she sighed. Was there really any better choice? She had a print of the Venetian canals above her bed that screamed romance.

He nodded.

'A definite possible. And in the meantime how about a trip to Bath next weekend?'

'I thought you had no desire to go back there.'

He shrugged.

'It's just the weekend. I'd really like you to meet Susie. She's got a weekend home from university. We could drive down and stay over.'

The enormity of what that meant made her heart turn softly over. Since the night in the hotel there had been no vague comments about when he might see her next, no talk of keeping things fun and no mention of no strings. He hadn't bailed the moment he bedded her. He couldn't have slept with her for a bet. She felt a stab of guilt now for ever harbouring that suspicion. He wasn't a player, not any more. He had proved it over and over again. With every new time she saw him her guard slipped that little bit more as he erased her insecurities.

Now King-of-the-One-Night-Stand Harry wanted to introduce her to his family. If she needed any further proof that he'd changed here it was.

'I'd love to,' she said.

He smiled in response, the gorgeous smile she loved that lifted the corner of his mouth and touched his blue eyes in crinkles at the corners. On impulse she leaned a little further, enough to kiss him. The gentle slide of his hands around her waist made her heartbeat speed up and then he was shifting his weight to one side and moving her gently onto her back. She looked up at him, her heart racing, her bones melting as he kissed her and his hands slid lower, finding bare skin beneath her clothes to stroke and caress until she was squirming with desire.

Afterwards she lay in his arms, his hand stroking her hair gently, her old throw tucked around them. The cosy darkness was broken only by the flickering light of the TV in the corner, with the sound turned off. She delighted in the languorous warmth, so comforting that she felt sated and sleepy. She couldn't remember the last time she'd felt this secure.

'Simon blamed social networking for what happened,' she said quietly into his shoulder. His skin was warm and smooth against her cheek; she picked up the faint citrus scent of his aftershave.

He frowned.

'Simon? Your ex?'

She nodded, concentrated on what she was saying. What she wanted to say. She'd fallen in love with him and her trust was completely his. This last thing she'd held back, she finally felt able to share. She'd coped with the past by bricking it up in her mind. Moving somewhere new, rebuilding herself. For a long time that had seemed the perfect solution.

Now she realised she'd been living her life to half its potential.

Putting the past in a box was not the same thing as letting it go; she knew that now. Boxing it up had been the perfect way of making it portable. She'd carried it all the way to London with her. What she needed was to really let it go instead of just kidding herself that she had. She wanted to look forward and confiding in Harry would be her first step in ceasing to look back.

'Social media sites, smartphones, all that kind of thing,' she said. 'It was just becoming popular when I was with Simon. No need to speak to someone face to face when you could do it virtually. Everyone was using it, posting messages, posting pictures.'

She gave a small bitter laugh.

'I don't even have an account now. Me, in Marketing, and I don't have a social media presence.'

'You're not making any sense,' he said gently. 'Did you discover he was having some kind of affair? Is that it?'

Alice shook her head, wishing it had been something so straightforward. Still a betrayal, of course, but maybe that level of humiliation might have been easier to rise above. She didn't move her head to look at him, stayed curled against him, fitting in the crook of his arm that was made for her, bare skin against his. It felt somehow easier to tell him if she didn't look into his eyes. She was afraid of what she might see there. She didn't want to feel stupid, the butt of a joke, not with him.

'Simon posted some photos,' she said, hearing the small click in her throat and trying hard to keep her voice neutral.

'Of what?'

'Of me.' She paused, wondering if he might get what she meant just from those two words. A quick glance up and she saw his eyes were filled with concern and something else. Anger.

'I let him take photos of me wearing...' She sighed against his shoulder. It sounded so damned *seedy* spoken out loud. 'Wearing hardly anything. And they ended up on the internet, viewed by all his friends, probably viewed by lots of people who weren't his friends too. In fact they're probably still lurking somewhere on the Net, still out there if you know how to use a search engine. There are sites, you know, where things like that end up.'

She closed her eyes briefly against him, her eyelashes faintly brushing his warm skin.

'I can't believe this,' he said. He sounded sickened.

'So now you know,' she said. 'Why I moved to London from Dorset. Why I find it so hard to take anyone at face value. Why I hadn't dated for three years. Why I tuned out everything apart from my career. Because at least in my job my success or failure is my own making, I don't need to worry about anyone else's meddling or intervention. That's why I found it so hard to believe you were anything more than your reputation. That's why I had you help me out at Tilly's face-painting party—I thought there was no way you'd be up for that if your only interest in me was sex. That's why I peered through your kitchen window when I thought you might be there with your ex instead of knocking on the front door and challenging you outright. Because the only explanation I could trust was one I found out for myself.'

Harry closed his hand over hers.

'Why didn't you tell me?'

She looked up at him then, her eyes wide, and his heart turned over softly in his chest.

'I don't tell anyone,' she said. 'I couldn't bear it when I found out what he'd done. The pictures had started to spread, people forwarded them like some hideous virus. Eventually someone took pity and let me know, but by then they were everywhere. It was harder to find one of our friends who hadn't seen them than one who had.'

She raked a hand through her hair, remembering.

'It was awful. Everyone looking at me, either pitying or leering. I haven't had to think about any of that since I moved here and it's been such a relief. That's why I haven't told anyone here, because I didn't want the whole circus to start up again.'

Dark anger boiled through Harry. If this Simon were to walk in the room now he knew he couldn't be held responsible for what he might do. Protectiveness of Alice so strong it made his heart contract combined with the desire to rip the man's head off for what he'd done to her. And then in the wake of that anger, the knowledge that he'd won the bet bore down on him again like a form of torture, a bomb ticking away beneath them. How long would this last between them if she were to find out he'd taken part in something so disrespectful?

He realised with a sickening lurch that he was pretty much cut from the same cloth. Sewer-rat, she'd called Simon. Well, he must be around that moral level too. She had lost the capacity to take a risk. Everything he'd said to her, every promise he made had to be double-checked. And after what had happened to her, who the hell could blame her for that? He could spend the rest of his days proving himself to her and it would be blown apart in an instant if she ever discovered the premise on which they'd got together.

He knew now what he'd found with her. Now that he knew how fragile it was. He was in love with her; he was happier than he could ever remember. And trust would be the thing on which they'd be broken. It filled him with despair.

If she found out about the bet now, it would ruin her.

A new day and he should be elated. New relationship. New life.

'There's still a faint whiff of prawns,' Alice said, walking into his sitting room with two steaming coffee mugs.

'You're imagining it,' he said.

She handed him one of the mugs.

'I'll buy you some scented candles.'

He pulled a face.

'Scented candles are only permissible if a girl lives on the premises,' he said.

She laughed.

She was barefooted and wearing one of his shirts, on her way upstairs to dress for work. The shirt gave a tantalising flash of creamy-smooth thigh that made him want to carry her straight back up to bed. Her hair was loose and she looked completely relaxed. She was a different person from the up-tight workaholic he'd followed into the office Ladies weeks ago. His heart twisted. He wanted things to stay this way. He wanted her belongings to start filtering into his house, their lives to become one.

Before he could look forward there was damage limitation.

He knew he had to be prepared to let all this go if he were to have the slimmest chance of keeping it.

* * *

Alone in his kitchen after she'd left for her early meeting, Harry forced himself to pull up the bet list on his laptop. He could hardly bear to look at it now; shame made his gut churn nauseatingly. The list made no reference whatsoever that this was a person's feelings they were betting on. How had he missed that? Had he disengaged himself so completely from caring about anyone else that he'd lost all sense of wrong and right? How could he have been so inconsiderate to her feelings?

He made a list of the participants and their bet amounts and tucked it into his wallet. Later today he would seek out each and every one of them and pay their stake money back, make it crystal clear that the bet was no longer on and that its existence was to be kept confidential.

If only he could be sure that was enough.

There was always the chance she might never find out. Part of him—the part that wanted to carry on being with her for ever, that wanted to protect her from the slightest thing that might cause her pain—wanted to grab that chance with both hands and run with it.

But it was unrealistic to think that he could remove all trace of the bet from their lives. It had been attached to numerous emails, was probably sitting in personal files on half the hard drives in the office; it might even be lurking somewhere in the office in print. Could he really risk Alice stumbling across it somewhere down the line? How could he live like that, loving her and waiting for that bomb to detonate?

Repaying the stakes and voiding the bet would be the easy part. He'd come to realise that the only real way to put this behind them was to tell Alice the whole truth. Yet after what had happened to her in the past, could he really expect their relationship to survive such a revelation?

Somehow he needed to find a way of coming clean to her that wouldn't make her hate him for the rest of her life.

Alice headed back to the office earlier than she'd expected. What a total waste of time that had turned out to be.

What was meant to be a meeting to sign off final logo designs had turned out to be a nightmare shift in the client's brief that sent the whole thing whizzing back to the drawing board.

She went straight up to the graphic design department to break the news to John that he was back to square one and the hours he'd already put in had come to nothing. There was a bit of a lull in the office as the lift opened and she checked her watch. Mid-morning, so half the staff were probably hanging around the coffee machine. The lack of background noise meant she was able to hear them before she turned the corner and saw them.

'I'm cancelling the whole thing. As of now,' Harry was saying.

Her heart give a tiny skip just at the sound of his voice. A smile rose on her lips as she picked up the pace, eager to see him although she'd only left his house a couple of hours earlier, and then faded away as her brain processed the conversation he was having.

'Cancelling the bet isn't an option,' John was saying. 'You can't just pull the plug. This isn't some high-street betting shop—it's a matter of honour. I know you think you're well in there with the Ice-Queen but I'm telling you, she was all over me at Roger's leaving do the other week and I deserve a crack at her. There's serious money riding on this, man.'

The floor felt suddenly unsteady beneath her feet, as if it were sand.

In disbelief she rounded the corner. Harry stood with his back to her, broad shoulders she'd been cuddled into just a few hours ago. John sat at his work station. As she watched Harry forked over a few banknotes onto the desk. John didn't pick them up. He'd caught sight of her and his rabbit-caught-in-headlights expression would have been priceless if her heart hadn't been breaking.

Harry turned to follow John's gaze and the colour drained from his face.

Shock slipped through her veins like ice. The need to find out every tiny, horrible, sinister detail blocked out every other thought.

'I want to see it,' she heard herself say.

'Alice…' Harry said, sounding sickened. 'I can explain. Let's go somewhere quiet, just the two of us—'

'I wasn't talking to you,' she snapped, not looking at Harry. Her voice sounded as if it was coming from a distance, not part of her at all. She looked at John, contempt flooding through her. 'You've got a copy of it, right? Unless you want to be sacked on the spot, show me the damn list!'

The open-plan office was broken up by room dividers and at the sound of her raised voice heads popped up like meer-cats to take in what was going on. Humiliation burned in her face at their interest and she fought the impulse to sprint from the office. Not this time. No crying in the Ladies for her any more; she was better than that.

After a glance at Harry during which he obviously decided his first loyalty was to his own pay packet, John made a few clicks on his computer and finally vacated his chair. She barely noticed him walk away as she sank into his chair and looked at the screen.

'Alice, don't,' Harry pleaded.

She ignored him. Because there it was.

The official Nail-Ice-Queen-Ford Betting Ring.

She scrolled down automatically to the bottom of the page and watched as the line continued. There was a Page Two after all. And there, a quarter of the way down, was his name. She looked at it, burning it into her brain as if staring at it might somehow make it disappear.

Harry Stephens.

And next to it, his stake. Two hundred pounds.

A quick scroll showed her his was the biggest stake of all. And that prompted her next move. A quick right click, a glance through Properties, and at last she knew everything. All the sickening details. The document was created by him. He'd not only organised the whole thing, he stood to gain the most from it too.

Correction. He *had* gained the most from it. Past tense. Because he'd won this thing a few weeks ago now. His winnings had probably more than covered the hotel bill for that first perfect night. Had he got some kind of hideous kick out of knowing that? It was that thought that punctured the calm and tipped her finally over the edge.

She felt the sudden lurching roll of nausea deep in her stomach, the wrenching contraction at the back of her throat. She clutched at her mouth with both hands and swallowed hard, gasping, forcing the hideous feeling back down, as if by controlling herself she might be able in some small way to retain control of the situation.

Some hope.

This situation was way past her redemption. And because she'd harboured suspicions for so long about him and then believed herself proven wrong it was somehow a million times worse. She'd known the full sweetness of relief as she let her guard down and put her trust in him, and the agony was all the more intense because he'd outwitted her. There'd been an ulterior motive all along. More fool her.

She looked up at Harry. He shook his head at her faintly, his expression despairing. She was dimly aware of her colleagues watching, soaking up the office joke. She should be used to it by now. The humiliation paled next to the total crushing defeat of his betrayal. She pushed back from the desk and stood up on shaky feet, held her head up high and walked from the room.

Harry followed her into her office, shut the door behind him and closed the blinds. None of which meant a thing. Outside that door she was gossip-central.

'Let me explain,' he said.

As if there could be an explanation?

'Explain?' she whispered. She could hear the desperation and disgust in her own voice. 'You organised a bet with your mates on who could get me into bed. You put the biggest damn stake of all on it yourself. You blagged your way into my life, you made me trust you, all in the name of getting the *proof required* for a cash win.'

Her voice was rising as anger began to seep in past the shock. Tears were here now, making her voice hitch. Her bag was on her desk and she grabbed it and hooked it over her shoulder, ready to leave.

'What was the proof, by the way?' she said. 'Did you come into work brandishing my underwear? Or maybe you took a photo of me sleeping.'

She was crying so much now that she could hardly see. 'What the hell kind of explanation can you possibly have?'

He sank both his hands into his hair and gazed desperately at her.

She wiped snot and tears from her face with the back of her hand. Her eyes felt swollen and scratchy.

'When I think back to that first day here in the Ladies, you made it seem like you were some kind of solution to all my problems. Like you were *helping* me.' She shook her head at the ceiling in disbelief. 'I'm such an idiot, buying into all of that.'

He reached out to take her hand and she snatched it away. 'Don't touch me!'

'I *did* want to help you,' he said. 'That was never a lie. I didn't like seeing you so unhappy.' A tortured frown touched his eyebrows as if he was thinking how to explain. 'I suppose what I was thinking, if I gave it a moment's consideration, was that it would be a win-win situation. We both have fun, you get back into dating again—'

'You win a wodge of cash,' she spat. 'Certainly a win for you. Really not sure now what the hell was in it for me. Or did you think that sleeping with you might be *enough* of a reward for me—is that it?'

'Alice, please…'

Harry clenched his fists with the sheer frustration of this because there was no way of explaining his way out of something so tacky. The fact he'd been intending to come clean would be no mitigation now.

'Do you know why I was crying in the Ladies that day?' she asked, her voice suddenly tinged with defeat. She didn't wait for his response. 'Of course you don't, because you never bothered to press further and find out once you'd got what you wanted out of the situation. I was crying because I found the first page of your bet list in one of the spare desks.'

A pause while she waited for that knowledge to sink in.

'Three years I've spent building a reputation at this company. Three years working hard and gaining respect instead of being known as a laughing stock. That's the thing with being publicly humiliated. After it happens it's the first thing people think of when they look at you. Doesn't matter what you do from then on, how good or clever or successful you are. You're always defined by that one hideous fact they have about you. That's what it was like back in Dorset. Why do you think I moved away and started again?'

He couldn't answer. What the hell could he say? The magnitude of what he'd done to her wasn't going to be smoothed over with a few apologetic sentences.

'Thanks to your pathetic, juvenile game I'm right the way back to square one.'

She paused for breath and looked at him steadily. He could hardly bear to look at the pain on her face, how pale she was, her eyes puffy and red-rimmed from all the crying.

'Alice, I'm sorry,' he said. 'Please just let me try and explain.'

She stood back and looked at him then with such coldness it tore at his heart.

'I don't know why you're so dead set on explaining and apologising,' she said. 'You won the bet. Why the hell should you care about the fallout? Or are you afraid that I might lob paint stripper over your car or start sending funeral wreaths to your address?'

'If it made things better I wish you would,' he said.

'Don't flatter yourself,' she said. 'I'll settle for never seeing you again.'

Sickening despair rose and sat in the pit of Harry's stomach like a stone, perspiration crept up his neck and his throat felt dry. The thought of being without her now filled him with crushing misery.

'We work together,' he said. 'You have to talk this through with me.'

'I don't have to do anything,' she said. 'And we won't be working together. I'm going to hand my notice in the first chance I get.'

He saw with sudden clarity how she was handling this.

'You're going to run away again, then?' he said.

'It worked before, didn't it?' she said. 'It was working perfectly well until you. I'll find another new town, another new job. And I won't make the same mistake next time.'

'Mistake?'

'Falling for you,' she spat. 'Goodness knows I was aware of the danger but I had to go and chance it anyway. Well, more fool me.'

She'd fallen for him.

The miserable ache that knowledge invoked made him gasp for breath as his throat constricted.

'Alice, I'm sorry,' he said. 'I truly was about to tell you.'

He knew how that sounded and her cynical snort told him he was spot on.

'I just bet you were.'

'I was.' He tried to hold her gaze so she would see he wasn't lying. She stared back at him and her look was pure hatred. He dropped his eyes because he couldn't stand it.

'This last week I've paid back every last person on that list. I've cancelled the bet. I wanted to undo as much damage as I could before I told you, so at least you would know it was over.'

'It's never going to be over,' she said.

He looked down at the floor.

'I know that,' he said. 'But no one stands to gain anything from it now, least of all me. I know that doesn't wipe away the fact that the thing existed in the first place but it's the best I could do. If I could go back and change things I would, but when it started I was up for a laugh, nothing more. That was the person I was then, the person I thought I wanted to be who didn't have to take anyone else's feelings into account.' He ran a hand through his hair. 'But then I got to know you. And now the thought that I've caused you so much pain is killing me. I was going to tell you about it. After you told me what your ex did I knew how much it would hurt you but I thought you would want me to be honest.'

She looked at him for a moment, then turned for the door.

'Alice, I love you,' he called after her, hearing the crack in his own voice.

She paused. A faint shred of hope lifted his heart. Maybe she would change her mind, give him the chance to talk her round properly.

Then she turned back to face him. Her face was pale and blotchy from the tears she'd shed but her expression was utterly resolute.

'I never want to see you again,' she said, and slammed the office door so hard on her way out that he almost felt the building shudder.

CHAPTER TWELVE

'A NUNNERY IT is, then, Sister Ford,' Tilly said.

Alice stared at the cup of coffee and the sandwich she didn't want, lying between them on the coffee-shop table. Normally she would have eaten lunch at her desk but the feeling, real or imagined, of being stared at in there was suffocating. Her declaration to Harry that she'd simply hand her notice in had been a heat-of-the-moment luxury. The reality was that she simply couldn't afford to walk out of her role at Innova, not without another post to go to. Tilly's offer of coffee was a welcome time-out.

She could have done without the side order of advice.

'Don't joke about it,' she said.

'I'm not joking. Well, not really. You're basically denouncing men for the rest of your days.'

'Not men. *A man.*'

'The one who says he loves you.'

She fought the urge to clap her hands over her ears and sing loudly to drown this out. She didn't need to hear Harry's declaration of love repeated by Tilly. She was having enough trouble squishing it out of her head as it was.

Oblivious, Tilly carried on, fighting Harry's corner when she was supposed to be in Alice's.

'OK, so what he did was terrible, but he was already doing everything he could to fix it, even before you found out about it. He paid back everyone who contributed to the pool—right? He said he was going to come clean to you. He's sorry. You're miserable without him. Where's your sense of forgiveness?'

'Simon used it up.'

Tilly threw a hand up.

'And there we are again. Simon's name comes back up. You're still letting what that moron did control your decisions.'

Alice flung exasperated hands up.

'You make it sound so easy. Let's all move on, never mind that the entire office is talking about me and laughing.'

'It'll be yesterday's news before you know it. The only person still dwelling on it will be you.'

'That's so easy for you to say, isn't it? Because you don't have to work there.'

Tilly shrugged.

'Neither do you. Look for another job. Take a sabbatical. Sweep it all under the carpet and run away from it like you did with Simon.' She leaned forward. 'Or you could ring the changes, stay put and brazen it out.'

'You're meant to be my friend—you're meant to be on my side.'

'I am. That's why I'm telling you this. I've never seen you as happy as you were those few weeks with him. It was like getting the old Alice back.' Tilly's gaze was gentle. 'Isn't that worth a second chance? You can come out of this situation in one of two ways, honey. You can carry on being the victim or you can rise above it.'

Alice stared into her coffee. She'd thought herself so empowered, making a new life after Simon's betrayal, controlling every tiny corner of it, reinventing herself as a single professional with no time for relationships, carving herself a niche where she could finally feel safe. Yet all the time every aspect of what she was doing was being driven by the very thing she wanted to put behind her. Moving to London had made no difference. She'd stayed the butt of Simon's joke for three years because she'd brought the effects of it right along with her.

Now she had Harry's betrayal to replace Simon's. A whole new nightmare to pick over, maybe for three more years, during which the thought of letting another man in filled her with dread.

And when you got past all the anger about the bet pool, lurking underneath was the aching, miserable loss of Harry and it took her breath away. She hadn't counted on enjoying his company so much, laughing with him, talking with him, making love with him. He had completed her one-sided life in a way she hadn't anticipated. And doing without him left a gaping, miserable emptiness that bravado simply wasn't enough to fill.

Tilly was right: becoming a nun was a pretty comparable alternative future.

She could let it go.

A few weeks ago that would have been unthinkable. But a few weeks ago she hadn't known Harry. Hadn't fully comprehended how destructive holding a grudge could be. Hadn't known the joy she was depriving herself of in the name of caution. OK, so she hadn't shredded Simon's clothes or filled his curtain rails with frozen prawns, but maybe if she had she might be in a healthier place now. Instead she'd turned her anger and hurt inwards and had carried it with her instead of getting over it.

She could do it all again. She could be the perpetual victim. Or—shock-horror—she could rise above it all and follow her own dreams instead of letting the past squash them.

The idea of being aloof and deprecating suddenly felt vaguely as if it might be very classy and grown-up.

She just wasn't sure if moving on and forgiving Harry could be the same thing.

Straight home from work yet again and then in for the evening.

For over a year now staying in had been pretty much unheard of. Even on weeknights. When he wasn't dating he was out with friends or colleagues, soaking up every social vibe London had to offer.

The thought of going out had no appeal whatsoever. He hadn't the remotest interest in the new intern who'd started this week at the office and whose skirt length should be illegal. What had Alice done to him?

All he could think about was what he'd lost. The feeling, suppressed so hard that he'd almost forgotten it, of being part of a team, of looking after someone and earning their love and respect. Of loving someone and having them love you in return. Being with Alice had felt like coming home.

The idea that he needed to be needed came as a shock, and the solution was never going to be found in London, not when seeing Alice every day reminded him what could have been.

He opened his laptop and drafted his resignation.

Pouring everything into work had been Alice's way of surviving after Simon's betrayal. Fourteen-hour days had leeched so much energy from her that she'd had little left for anything else. She didn't even have that this time—how could she lose herself in work when everyone she dealt with there had been in on the joke? She withdrew back to keeping all her workmates at a completely professional distance. No room for small talk or friendly conversation.

She kept out of Harry's way—not that it was difficult. He

seemed to have ceased all socialising. There were no more crying assistants. He came into work, did his job, went home again. And avoiding him like the plague seemed to be helping, right up until she saw his job advertised on the internal notice board.

He was leaving.

As he opened the door of his office in response to her knock her heart, steeled against any rash impulses, turned softly over. Up close he didn't look like someone who was living it up on a diet of no-strings flings any more. He looked a bit like she felt. Tired and pale. Sleep hadn't been a friend to her these past days.

'Alice!'

Genuine surprise.

'Can we talk?'

He opened the door wider and stood well back, careful not to be in her personal space, yet still she was acutely aware of him as she stepped past him into the room. A quick glance sideways showed a resigned expression in his blue eyes.

'Coffee?' he asked her, as if they had never been anything more than colleagues. She shook her head and sat down by the desk.

'I heard you handed in your notice,' she said.

He closed the door and crossed the room to sit behind the desk as if this were some work meeting.

'I'm moving back towards Bath. Thinking of doing some freelance work for a while.' He paused. 'And I thought it might be easier for you if I'm not around.'

He was thinking of her. London party animal Harry was prepared to exit his life so that she might breathe a bit easier in hers.

'I thought this was your big escape route,' she said. 'Now you tell me you're going back home.'

He was looking downwards and she saw a smile touch his lips.

'You're right, I did move to London to escape. But it turns out you can't just chop chunks out of your life and become a different person. I spent so long looking out for Susie and my mum it must have become ingrained. I'm not sure what my purpose is here any more.'

'You could still stay in London,' she said. 'Even if you left Innova you could find another job. You're great at what you do. I'm sure it wouldn't take you long.'

He looked up at her then, the blue eyes clear, and shook his head.

'I miss it,' he said. 'I was so busy resenting the way my family tied me down and made demands on me that I overlooked what *I* was getting from *them*. Having someone to care about and look out for, that feeling of belonging. I didn't even realise I missed it until I got to know you. I'd convinced myself the single life was so great. Then I met you, I fell for you, and now I've lost you. And I feel…' he looked up at the ceiling as if searching for the right word '…rootless. There's nothing here for me any more.' He shook his head wonderingly. 'I was so afraid I was like my father deep down because all I used to think about was getting away. Turns out, getting away wasn't all it was cracked up to be.'

'I told you before, you've always been different from your father. You might have felt like you were being held back but you didn't act on that. You made a choice to stay and look after your family. You're not him. You're better than that.'

He offered her a small smile.

'Thanks.'

'So it really will be over, then, once you've gone.'

The thought of that finality, of knowing that she really wouldn't see him again, brought a wave of regret. All that potential happiness just gone in one fell swoop.

He nodded.

'Yes, it will be over. I'm so sorry, Alice, for what happened, for the way I treated you. I've done as much as I can to put it right but without turning back time it was never going to be enough, was it? I just hope you can be happy going forward and maybe one day you can forgive me.'

The tortured look in his eyes wrenched at her heart.

He was moving away. He'd disbanded the bet pool so no one would benefit from it and now he was leaving his job, leaving London. She would never see him again. She searched again for the satisfaction in that and found none. The hideous ache of losing him hurt far more than the stupid bruised pride the bet had caused.

She was through caring what people thought of her. Where had it ever got her?

'I was over the bet weeks ago, Harry,' she said. 'In a way I began to see it as a positive thing—I was floundering along living half a life, pouring everything into work and spending my evenings like some recluse. I'm only twenty-seven, for goodness' sake. Life was passing me by. It was the kick up the butt I needed to get me out of that rut.'

'I still don't get the feeling you're about to thank me for it.'

She grinned ruefully at that.

'Don't push your luck,' she said.

She saw the tiniest spark in his blue eyes interrupt the flat defeat of his gaze.

'I carried on working with all the people on that list, knowing I was the butt of gossip. At the beginning I had no idea if you were on the list or not. It really didn't matter then. What mattered was that by dating you I was proving everyone wrong and building up a bit of a social life for myself.'

She looked across the desk at him. 'You weren't the only one with a hidden agenda.'

She watched him frown as that statement kicked in.

'What do you mean a hidden agenda?'

'When you offered to take me out as some kind of integration back into dating, my first instinct was to turn you down flat. But then I thought it over and I decided it might be a good thing. You were the exact type of guy I wanted to avoid. So I came up with a list of rules that I thought would define a player. Traits that I remembered from when I dated Simon. Like the fact a player would move things on to the physical as fast as possible because getting laid would be his main aim. And a player wouldn't really be interested in getting to know me, just in getting his hands on me. I thought I could come up with some kind of profile and then I'd be equipped to avoid that kind of relationship in the future. I could weed out the dross.' She paused. 'And I thought I could test the theory on you.'

The look on his face was incredulous.

'You were using me to come up with some behaviour sketch? What kind of ludicrous amateur psychology is that?'

She could hear a twinge of indignation in his voice and defensiveness immediately kicked in. He was *so* not having the moral high ground. Not now.

'I know it sounds a bit off the wall. But I liked the idea of having some concrete rules to follow instead of just relying on my own judgement of character. Let's face it, I hadn't exactly had great success at that in the past.'

'But still…' He pulled a face. 'A list of rules?'

'It turned out to be my downfall,' she said. 'You started out proving my point with that tried-and-tested boating-lake date but then somewhere along the way you started flouting the profile at every turn. Walking away after kissing me when my rules said that you should be falling over yourself to get me upstairs to bed. Letting me paint your face and stepping in at a kids' party when my rules said that you should have been steering way clear of anything outside your comfort zone. And the more rules you bent, the more I began to believe you weren't really a player after all. You were a keeper, you just didn't know it.'

She sighed.

'And that was why it was so devastating, Harry, finding out *you* were behind that stupid bet. Because you'd proved me wrong again and again and again. And then, when I'd finally let myself be convinced you didn't deserve your awful reputation, began to believe we might have a future, it turned out that the entire relationship was underpinned by this big lie.'

He was shaking his head.

'The rule thing is totally crazy,' he said.

She smiled a little.

'Maybe it is. It didn't do me any good. Growing up I felt so dispensable. Neither of my parents ever really needed me. If I'm honest, really honest, I tried to turn my relationship with Simon into more than it really was because I wanted that feeling of belonging somewhere. To him it was just a light-hearted fling but to me it was about being needed. After I moved here I couldn't face another relationship so I tried to make myself indispensable at work instead. I like that feeling of being wanted.'

She shrugged and stole a glance at him. He was looking at her intently.

'Unfortunately I ended up channelling needy instead. I should have been letting go of the past, taking new people at face value, but instead I was there with a big fat list of rules defining you by what happened to me before. I'm tired of it, Harry. I just want to let it go.'

She looked up at him and suddenly he was out of his chair and around the desk in a few quick paces. He knelt in front of her and took both her cold hands in his own.

'You *can* let it go. We're not so different. We've both tried to freeze out big aspects of our lives because we thought that's what it would take to be happy. I cut my family out and you swore off men. It didn't work. We ended up living half a life, both of us held back by what happened in the past instead of letting it go.'

He squeezed her hands gently.

'If you can forgive me we could try again. Just look forward instead of back. I promise you, I'll never let you down again. I'll never hide anything from you or do anything but protect you.'

He looked openly into her face, holding her gaze with clear blue eyes that were filled with nothing but love and concern. She felt her love for him. The thought of a future ahead of her without him in it filled her with despair. It was the safe option, of course, no fear of betrayal or loss if she put an end to it right now. She could put in for another promotion at work, maybe think about buying a house instead of renting. She would still be upwardly mobile; she didn't need a man to be that.

But he was right: she would be living half a life.

'I did everything I could think of to put things right,' he went on. 'If I could give you my head on a pole I would. I'm so sorry, Alice.'

She swallowed hard to get rid of a sudden dry sensation at the back of her throat.

Harry saw the hesitation in her eyes and his heart twisted.

'You haven't quite done everything possible to put it right,' she said, lifting her chin in the cute way she had that made him want to kiss her and kiss her and kiss her. Thinking that gesture wouldn't be for him from now on filled him with misery.

'How do you mean?'

'The money,' she said.

He stared at her.

'The money?'

'Yes. I want the money. The stake money you were in line to win by sleeping with me.' She took one of her hands away and examined her fingernails, not looking at him. 'I think I've earned it.'

'I cancelled the bet,' he said. Did she not understand how these things worked? 'I paid everyone their stake back. The bet pool is empty.'

'Then you'll have to cover all the stake money yourself,' she said airily. 'The whole pool. Winner takes all. I've seen the list so I should be in line for a few hundred quid.'

So that was it.

'Enough money to sweeten a new start, is that it?' he said. 'Compensation.'

'Something like that.'

She'd come here for money? Not to talk. Then there had never been any hope at all.

As if in a dream he stood up, went to the desk drawer and took out his chequebook. When he'd written and signed a cheque he tore it out and turned to see that she was standing up. Ready to leave. He fought the feeling of impending emptiness and held the cheque out to her.

'Thanks,' she said, folding it.

He pre-empted her and walked towards the door, the depth of his sadness making his throat dry and his limbs ache.

'I'll put it towards Venice,' she said from behind him.

His heart gave a tiny cautious jolt.

'Venice?'

He turned slowly around.

'Yes,' she said and shrugged. 'I figure since I wasn't exactly straight with you about my list of rules, and since I've now won the bet myself, that just about makes us even.'

He searched her face for some sign that she was joking. She was looking at him steadily. His heartbeat was climbing towards breakneck.

'A new start. You, me, no past baggage and Venice. What do you say?'

She smiled her cute smile at him and he let himself believe. Relief and excitement flooded in. He couldn't say anything. Instead he pulled her into his arms. She tangled her hands in his hair.

'You sure Venice is a good choice?' he whispered, between melting kisses, not caring who might walk in.

'Romantic capital of the world,' she said. 'What's not to like?'

He kissed his way slowly along her jaw.

'I wasn't thinking about that,' he said, moving his lips to brush her neck. She squirmed deliciously against him. 'More about your track record with boats.'

ALICE FORD'S DATING CRITERIA
Rule #12 Disregard rules 1-11. Truth is, there are no rules.

* * * * *

Mills & Boon® Hardback
August 2013

ROMANCE

The Billionaire's Trophy	Lynne Graham
Prince of Secrets	Lucy Monroe
A Royal Without Rules	Caitlin Crews
A Deal with Di Capua	Cathy Williams
Imprisoned by a Vow	Annie West
Duty At What Cost?	Michelle Conder
The Rings that Bind	Michelle Smart
An Inheritance of Shame	Kate Hewitt
Faking It to Making It	Ally Blake
Girl Least Likely to Marry	Amy Andrews
The Cowboy She Couldn't Forget	Patricia Thayer
A Marriage Made in Italy	Rebecca Winters
Miracle in Bellaroo Creek	Barbara Hannay
The Courage To Say Yes	Barbara Wallace
All Bets Are On	Charlotte Phillips
Last-Minute Bridesmaid	Nina Harrington
Daring to Date Dr Celebrity	Emily Forbes
Resisting the New Doc In Town	Lucy Clark

MEDICAL

Miracle on Kaimotu Island	Marion Lennox
Always the Hero	Alison Roberts
The Maverick Doctor and Miss Prim	Scarlet Wilson
About That Night...	Scarlet Wilson

Mills & Boon® Large Print
August 2013

ROMANCE

Master of her Virtue	Miranda Lee
The Cost of her Innocence	Jacqueline Baird
A Taste of the Forbidden	Carole Mortimer
Count Valieri's Prisoner	Sara Craven
The Merciless Travis Wilde	Sandra Marton
A Game with One Winner	Lynn Raye Harris
Heir to a Desert Legacy	Maisey Yates
Sparks Fly with the Billionaire	Marion Lennox
A Daddy for Her Sons	Raye Morgan
Along Came Twins…	Rebecca Winters
An Accidental Family	Ami Weaver

HISTORICAL

The Dissolute Duke	Sophia James
His Unusual Governess	Anne Herries
An Ideal Husband?	Michelle Styles
At the Highlander's Mercy	Terri Brisbin
The Rake to Redeem Her	Julia Justiss

MEDICAL

The Brooding Doc's Redemption	Kate Hardy
An Inescapable Temptation	Scarlet Wilson
Revealing The Real Dr Robinson	Dianne Drake
The Rebel and Miss Jones	Annie Claydon
The Son that Changed his Life	Jennifer Taylor
Swallowbrook's Wedding of the Year	Abigail Gordon

0713 GEN STD LP

Mills & Boon® Hardback
September 2013

ROMANCE

Challenging Dante	Lynne Graham
Captivated by Her Innocence	Kim Lawrence
Lost to the Desert Warrior	Sarah Morgan
His Unexpected Legacy	Chantelle Shaw
Never Say No to a Caffarelli	Melanie Milburne
His Ring Is Not Enough	Maisey Yates
A Reputation to Uphold	Victoria Parker
A Whisper of Disgrace	Sharon Kendrick
If You Can't Stand the Heat...	Joss Wood
Maid of Dishonour	Heidi Rice
Bound by a Baby	Kate Hardy
In the Line of Duty	Ami Weaver
Patchwork Family in the Outback	Soraya Lane
Stranded with the Tycoon	Sophie Pembroke
The Rebound Guy	Fiona Harper
Greek for Beginners	Jackie Braun
A Child to Heal Their Hearts	Dianne Drake
Sheltered by Her Top-Notch Boss	Joanna Neil

MEDICAL

The Wife He Never Forgot	Anne Fraser
The Lone Wolf's Craving	Tina Beckett
Re-awakening His Shy Nurse	Annie Claydon
Safe in His Hands	Amy Ruttan

Mills & Boon® Large Print
September 2013

ROMANCE

A Rich Man's Whim	Lynne Graham
A Price Worth Paying?	Trish Morey
A Touch of Notoriety	Carole Mortimer
The Secret Casella Baby	Cathy Williams
Maid for Montero	Kim Lawrence
Captive in his Castle	Chantelle Shaw
Heir to a Dark Inheritance	Maisey Yates
Anything but Vanilla...	Liz Fielding
A Father for Her Triplets	Susan Meier
Second Chance with the Rebel	Cara Colter
First Comes Baby...	Michelle Douglas

HISTORICAL

The Greatest of Sins	Christine Merrill
Tarnished Amongst the Ton	Louise Allen
The Beauty Within	Marguerite Kaye
The Devil Claims a Wife	Helen Dickson
The Scarred Earl	Elizabeth Beacon

MEDICAL

NYC Angels: Redeeming The Playboy	Carol Marinelli
NYC Angels: Heiress's Baby Scandal	Janice Lynn
St Piran's: The Wedding!	Alison Roberts
Sydney Harbour Hospital: Evie's Bombshell	Amy Andrews
The Prince Who Charmed Her	Fiona McArthur
His Hidden American Beauty	Connie Cox